"Dog, It's Kiss-Your-Ass-Goodbye Time..."

"It's been fun," Stone said, reaching down and giving a quick scratch behind the animal's ear. Then they charged down the stairs, leaping over the bikes and the dead.

Just beyond was the main computer center. Stone's jaw hung open as he came tearing in. This must have been the center of the entire space fleet—and the Dwarf had control of it. Surely the gods had gone mad.

Anyone who was trying to blow up the world was fair game in Stone's book. He ran down the huge complex, firing at everything including technicians at various posts. His slugs rocked them from their seats. Suddenly Stone saw him ahead—the Dwarf, racing down a row of control panels in his wheelchair, punching out at rows of buttons and dials with an absolutely maniacal expression on his face. Stone prayed it wasn't already too late, that this wasn't the final launch sequence that Dwarf was punching in.

He ran down the central aisle of the place, firing, holding the trigger and letting loose with a barrage...

D1737869

IS THIS THE END?

CRAIG SARGENT

POPULAR LIBRARY

An Imprint of Warner Books, Inc.

A Warner Communications Company

POPULAR LIBRARY EDITION

Cover illustration by Norm Eastman

Popular Library books are published by
Warner Books, Inc.
666 Fifth Avenue
New York, N.Y. 10103

 A Warner Communications Company

Printed in the United States of America

First Printing: January, 1989

10 9 8 7 6 5 4 3 2 1

CHAPTER
One

THEY were the the ugliest of men. Freaks of nature, mutilated caricatures of how men should look. Dwarfs with twisted limbs, burned men whose flesh was nothing but bubbles and boils, albinos with pink eyes, skin as white as chalk, and not a hair on their baby-smooth bodies, a man with dark green scales that covered every inch of him, yet another with a grotesque blood-colored tumor six inches long which grew from out of the top of his forehead. And others no less hideous. Yet they were unconcerned with their ugliness. It meant nothing, less than nothing to abominations such as these. If anything it was a tool for them, for it created fear and confusion in other men and gave the freaks power over them. Power meant all in their world. And in their own dark way, though few even knew of their existence, they were living proof that the brain, the will, are all that matter. The flesh is secondary. It is the mind that rules men.

They sat on widely varied shapes and sizes of chairs— made of metals, plastics, foam—designed to fit each of their specific bodily contours. For each was distinctly different in size and shape. The ten freaks formed a circle around a pulsing electronic map of the U.S. set into the top of the twenty-foot wide oval-shaped table at which they sat. The map blinked and lit up everywhere as they eyed it with interest, digesting the information it displayed concerning their empire of criminal operations throughout America. Though an outsider, if he didn't faint from sheer fear, wouldn't have been able to discern the slightest sign of emotion from the misshapen men; they had all met in this central information room enough times over the past years to know one another intimately. It was known that the twist of the Dwarf's mouth, the set of the albino's eye, the coloration of the red horn-like tumor meant a particular emotional state. Thus they studied each other closely for the slightest clues without letting on that they were, though all knew that was just what was occurring. They were searching for clues that would help them gain some advantage in the Game, the Game that they all lived for. The Game of power.

"Gentlemen," an armless and legless dwarf spoke up in a high-pitched voice that was grating to the others, though none dared speak a word of protest. "We see before us a great evolution in the Game, a quantum leap, dare I say. For all these lights flickering before us are ours now. Look you of the Ten. Look and savor our accomplishments." There was a reverential silence for a few seconds as they all glanced around at the computerized electronic map which lit up the center of the table with a brilliant glow. The map was contoured and colored as it actually appeared from space, with mountains that rose up several inches and rivers that almost appeared by the quality of their tinted plastic to be flowing. But it wasn't the shapes or colorations of the multimillion dollar map that caught their eyes, rather it was the vast number of amber lights that outlined their domain.

The amber blinking dots were everywhere on the map. From coast to coast they twinkled like stars of pure wealth, the chickens that laid the golden eggs. But these golden eggs were ripped from the already savaged populations— and the chickens were drugs, liquor, and women. The drug dealers and whorehouses that they controlled around America, a vast hidden but intertwined criminal empire, dwarfed anything the Mafia had ever dreamed of. Though there were blue lights for the Mafia operations, and for the biker gangs red, along with a smattering of green, yellow, and other lights representing the other major competing murder inc.'s who were all trying to struggle bloodily to the top. But the Ten were way ahead, far ahead. And the map showed it. Numbers didn't lie. And their amber lights were like a galaxy now, absorbing the other colors everywhere around the map.

"As you can see," the Dwarf squealed, sitting in the highest chair, both to be seen and because, although they were all theoretically equal in power and vote, the Dwarf was still the power behind the power, officially unacknowledged—but also unchallenged. "We've made a surge forward in the last few months, since our last full Tribunal meeting." Smiles crossed twisted faces. "Our holdings have nearly doubled and our drug operations have reached out to create and feed vast numbers of addicts. Life is hard in the badlands—we help to ease that pain. And we are being richly rewarded for our efforts."

"It is time. Time to strike now!" the scale-faced man spoke up with a rasping sound as if he had a tongue made of bone instead of flesh. "Time to claim what is ours by virtue of our strength, our will to power."

"No, no, not yet!" the Dwarf squealed back, squirming around in his motorized .50-caliber machine gun armed and armored wheelchair with rows of buttons along each armrest which he could manipulate with the purple stumps of his arms. "We could lose all by moving too soon. We're just beginning to truly consolidate our power. Look around the board." All eyes turned back again and grew silent as the Dwarf poked at one of the buttons on his panel and the wheelchair began moving around behind them. He spoke as the chair whirred and though all heads remained focused on the electronic map, their backs rippled with shivers as the egg-shaped man went by. None of them trusted him worth a damn even though they allowed him to be head of the council of Ten. But then none of them trusted any of the others worth a damn either. Years of assassinations, poisonings, betrayals and constantly changing alliances had reduced their original numbers down to these ten. Now a sort of balance of power, balance of terror, had been achieved.

"Look! Look at the board," the Dwarf shrieked out. "Yes, we have many lights there. But so do others. Perhaps we are even the strongest now. But if the rest feel that we pose a threat to take the whole pie—I promise you whatever alliances we have worked out with them all will tear apart like flesh in a vulture's beak. We cannot afford to take them all on. To allow a war to break out now—we would lose—whatever the rest of you believe. Do not be too greedy. Our ten year plan is developing at an accelerated pace. We will have it all. Never fear. What is the sound of a civilization collapsing?" the Dwarf cackled as he completed his circumference of the table and came back to his place.

"The snapping teeth of the predators who feed upon her," he answered his own death riddle. "There is plenty to feast upon in America. And there is time to do it."

"That's easy for you to say." Scarma, the radiation-burned freak spoke up from his side of the table as all eyes shifted to him. None, even the foulest of them, enjoyed looking into that molten face with teeth hanging out of his mouth as if on strips of taffy, nose dripping down around the left cheek, ears melted down to little pinholes around which mounds of lumpy flesh custard sat. This, plus his total hairlessness and single eye (the other was now the consistency of charcoal and sat like a dead thing in his face) made even the Dwarf tremble slightly when gazing on the melted features. "*You're* winning in the Game now, Dwarf. It is to your advantage to have this thing be drawn out. That's the way your approach works, Dwarf, slow and deep, like poison administered over years. But we others have our own approaches. I prefer the blitzkrieg mode. Strike fast, strike hard—before they know what hit them."

There was a murmuring among them as they looked

around trying to gauge clues as to each of the men's thoughts on this issue before they committed themselves. They were the most consummate of politicians, most of them ready to change as readily as the wind changes, depending on their self interest and the prevailing power. The Dwarf was the power now but he knew that he would be challenged. He had been challenged before though all who had tried were dead. For a man without arms or legs, weighing less than eighty pounds, the Dwarf was able to inspire fear and dread in the hardest of men.

Suddenly there was a buzz on the intercom units built into the table, and a voice spoke out.

"Security Chief Hopkins here—the prisoners are ready."

"Bring them in," the Dwarf hissed into the recessed receiver before the others had a chance to say a thing. It was an opportunity to break off discussion of the country-wide situation, which was to the Dwarf's advantage. Within seconds the thick metal doors of the immense high tech communications room they sat in whooshed open with puffs of air on their hidden hydraulic systems, and two men wearing green uniforms with their rank insignias torn off the shoulders, leaving bald empty spots that bespoke crimes—and punishments—came in. The two, eyes brimming over with terror-squeezed tears, were marched to one side of the table between four submachine-gun-toting beefy MP's also with the same green uniforms, but these with the letters N.A.U.A.S.C. still on them. The men's hands were bound behind their backs by plastic ties, their ankles as well, making them walk in short little steps like a Chinese woman of old with wrapped feet. They were as trapped as roaches in a roach motel. And they knew it.

Just seeing the faces of the Ten made the prisoners freeze up and avert their eyes. Most of the men of the complex didn't get to see the Tribunal, who preferred to remain on one side of the steel wall that stretched through the vast underground cavern, perhaps because of their deformities —or just because they felt safer deep underground, hidden away like slugs beneath impenetrable logs. In any case, the effect of seeing all ten freaks of nature at once was almost too much for both men and their hearts began palpitating wildly within their chests.

"What is the sound a thief makes?" the Dwarf asked, wheeling around in his motorized chair, "when he is caught?" He rode up to them and stopped a few feet away, wanting to look into their eyes to see the fear in them, feed upon it the way a leech feeds on blood. For the Dwarf took great pleasure in the fear of others, in the terror of those who knew they were about to die. And these were such. He wanted to know those eyes, know the men, the way one wants to know a lover, so that when he killed them he would be able to touch that presence called a soul inside of them and see it vanish like smoke. For this was the Dwarf's greatest pleasure—watching men's souls disappear like blood-colored soap bubbles popping their invisible contents into empty air.

"Please, please," one of the men said, the shorter of the two, his face a mass of bruises, some teeth knocked out where the guards had had their fun back in the steel-walled cells, where they had spent the last six days thinking about what they had done. "We meant no harm. Only took a bottle for ourselves—not to sell or nothing."

"It is the sound of pleading," the Dwarf answered his own question. "The begging of a man like yourself, trying to think of any way that he can convince those who hold the power of life and death over him that he is innocent—and should be spared." The man's mouth froze. The fucking Dwarf had him pegged too well. And he didn't at all like the way the shrunken egg man was looking at him, like a rat looking down at a sleeping baby's cheeks.

"You have been accused of stealing four bottles of liquor from the NAUASC stocks. You know the punishment for such a crime. The rules are clear down here. Signs are posted everywhere detailing correct—and all that is incorrect—behavior."

"My God—my wife, my children," the other younger and taller man began whispering through teeth that were clenched so tightly he could barely be heard even by the ultra-sensitive ears of the tumor-headed man that could hear a pin drop at a hundred feet.

"They will be used, do not worry," the Dwarf hissed as he wriggled around in his seat trying to get more comfortable. The four stumps of his missing appendages sometimes grew swollen, and hurt as if they were rippled with fire, as they did today. And the Dwarf's growing excitement at the imminent fates of the two men seemed to make them swell even more and throb with painful waves.

"No," the Dwarf went on, his voice growing higher-pitched with every word. "Your guilt is proven—the bottles were found with you—half drunk. The penalty is unequivocal and irreversible."

"No, God no," both men whispered as neither could even quite get up the energy to scream anymore. They were already beaten down into states of near mindlessness.

"Yes, yes," the Dwarf mocked their words. "The fate is sealed in blood. You must die. Both of you. And right now. Are you ready to go? Ready to see what lies beyond the veiled curtain, what lies beyond the screams and the blood."

"No!" the short one cried out. "No! No! No!" over and over in staccato delivery. The guards were pulling back from both sides of the men and they both suddenly noticed that the guards were standing ten feet away. The Dwarf locked eyes on the younger one with wife and child. He was the more interesting of the two. His soul would have more substance because he wanted so desperately to live. The Dwarf seemed to go almost into trance as the prisoner's eyes were caught by his mad gaze and became hypnotized, unable to turn away.

The Dwarf stabbed out with his left stump at a black button and a radio signal sent out the "go" command. Instantly the entire hundred by seventy-five-foot chamber bounded on all sides by smooth steel walls was filled with a bright, nearly blinding light. The freaks had to squint through their half-closed eyes to see though they could hear

the screams clearly enough. Streaks of electricity were ripping from floor to ceiling and going through the men to
complete their arcs, for the two were standing on steel
plates hidden beneath the fine tapestry rug. Similar plates
were on the ceiling twenty feet above as well.

The men were performing a most horrible dance, a ma-
cabre imitation of anything graceful. The electricity tore
through them, their hands and arms snapped out wildly like
chickens with broken wings, as their heads spun around on
their necks as if trying to rip themselves off. Their legs
were moving like jackhammers, as both men bounced
around in place as if pogo sticks had been shoved up their
asses.

They screamed for a split second as it first hit but
quickly stopped as megavolts of current made all the muscles in their bodies clench and unclench many times a second. It was as if they were computer controlled
puppets—only the computer had gone mad and didn't
quite know which way to move them, so it kept changing
their motions over and over as if trying out a thousand
different patterns every second. Their faces almost lit up
from within as if they had lights in their chests, and a glow
emitted from their mouths and within their eyes. But only
for a few seconds. Then they began smoking. A thin bluish
smoke at first which rose up from ears and noses, between
lips. Within seconds it grew much thicker and darker with
a foul oily smell, like something long rotten was burning
on the stove.

The Dwarf's eyes were locked onto the jumping men's
own wide orbs filled with a terror beyond terror, a pain of
infinities. He watched as the flesh writhed in agony,
watched the eyes grow like they were about to burst, and
then as the fire within began consuming the body whole-
sale and it seemed to shrivel up beneath the skin, brown-
ing, the men's eyes grew very small. And the Dwarf
followed, went in with those eyes, saw them extinguish
and tried to grab hold of the bubble of the soul as it rose up
and away. He felt it for a second, and tried to catch a ride,

a thrill, like some super drug. But he couldn't quite get atop the thing. And it seemed to float away, not fast or in any great hurry, but slippery, intangible already.

A look of supreme satisfaction swept over the Dwarf's face for having felt it for even an instant—the death of a man. Suddenly the two corpses burst into open flame everywhere on their bodies. But still the electric bolts drove on, cracking and moving around the two smoking, jerking shapes like they were torching every cell of them. The bodies blackened to the color and texture of charcoal, and as the yellow flames swept through them, even what was left began disintegrating. Within two minutes from onset of power they were hardly more than burnt husks that vibrated in the air.

The Dwarf stabbed out again at the control panel and then let himself fall back into his seat drained. The electricity stopped instantly and the remains fell with hardly a sound as there was nothing solid enough left to make such noise. The Ten basked in the vision of the glowing remains for several minutes as normal men might bask in a sunset or a mountain vista. Theirs was the beauty of pain, the aesthetic of blood.

"Take the remains away," the Dwarf said after a few minutes. The MP's came forward and began vacuuming up the corpse powder into huge industrial bags. "Take what's left out into the main hall. Put them each in their own stainless steel urn, side by side. And a sign above them: 'These two broke the Rules of Assured Survival.' And get a new rug from supply—make it a nice dhurrie, something blue. I'm tired of this brown."

CHAPTER

Two

MARTIN Stone stared down at the pit bull on the back of his Harley. The dog looked like it was dead, or damn near it. Nothing was moving on the animal, not a breath, or muscle quivering. It had been like this for days now in a sort of coma as if it were waiting for Stone to fix it up again, repair the knife wound into its heart that it had taken fighting at his side two days before. Saving his life was more like it.

"Come on dog," Stone whispered through jaws clenched hard so his feelings wouldn't rise up. The very fact that he felt so much for the damn dog made him feel like an idiot in a way. On the other hand he trusted the animal more than most of the people he'd met these days. "Come on Excaliber," he said again, scratching the motionless animal as it lay sideways half curled up inside a low steel box carrier he had rigged up on the back rack of his Harley 1500. "You can make it." He didn't know if the animal could hear him or not. But it couldn't hurt to give the pit bull a little attention. Too bad there weren't any nurses around, that would surely have gotten the creature's heart fluttering a little as it had a way with the fair sex most men would envy.

The stitching along the pit bull's chest seemed to be holding up well enough, and as far as Stone could see no infection had set in. It looked red along the eighteen stitches that it had taken to open and close the canine's chest. But the man who had done the slicing had told him redness was normal. The once doctor had gone right in there and actually touched the animal's heart. Stone had seen it with his own eyes, the dog's living, beating heart being held in the "doctor's" hands as he had repaired the slice along one side. It had seemed like a terrible violation of the animal's body, which it was—but it had also kept him alive, though just how long the pit bull was going to stay in that condition was a question Stone didn't want to think too hard about.

He put his head down until it was just touching the dog's, and closed his eyes trying in some ridiculous telepathic way to establish some sort of contact with the dog. Let it know that he was still out there trying to get it all together. He knew he must be imagining it but somehow he felt for a few seconds like he was in contact with the pit bull and it was—if not ready to do the turkey trot—still hanging in there. It was almost as if it were in some kind of suspended animation with its every bodily function slowed down to a crawl. Maybe it was a defense mechanism that the breed had to protect itself. He knew that every other trait Excaliber had been given via his bloodline made him about as tough as living things could get. Maybe the dog had a built-in hibernation mode as well. Giving Stone a chance to. . . . To what? Damned if he even knew what the hell he could do beyond what had already been done.

He lifted his head from the comatose animal and raised it up toward the low-flying mountain-sized clouds. It had been getting darker all afternoon, but now as Stone's eyes scanned the heavens, he saw that even the glow of the sun had pretty much disappeared. Though it was only three in the afternoon it seemed to be night, a sickly night with a greenish tint to the entire sky as if it was made of mold. Stone felt a strange sensation sweep through his whole body, like he was holding his finger in a socket. He glanced down to see that the dog's hair was all standing on end, pricked up by the charge in the air. Something was up—and it wasn't a winning lottery ticket.

Even as he walked back to the front of the bike and mounted up, the heavens seemed to grow a few shades darker and a ghastlier green, almost like the face of a corpse, which Stone had unfortunately been seeing a lot of these days. Faces that didn't die in peace and sink into the ground but followed him into his dreams, all mixing and blending together into one great entity—the sky itself perhaps. It looked like it was rotting, falling down in chunks onto the earth below. The air was oppressive, hard to breathe, as if he were deep underground and there was no oxygen. Stone started the Harley forward, moving slowly as he didn't want to be caught unawares going any real speed.

He had barely gotten up to about twenty miles per hour when the whole horizon lit up with a thousand streaks of lightning, blinding Stone. He had to slow down fast and throw both feet down onto the ground to keep upright. The spears of lightning sparked and bolted in all directions, but he was able to see by cupping one hand over his eyes and squinting. It looked like all hell was breaking loose as the clouds were being whipped around by frenzied winds. They broke into massive sections and flew around wildly like fish seeking deeper waters. The winds picked up fast, thirty, then forty miles an hour at least. And the loose sand from the flatlands he was traveling through whipped up all around him, flying into the front of the bike and his face and chest like the grains were bent on annihilation. Stone had to bend his whole body forward to keep from being blown over. He pulled some goggles he had around his neck over his eyes and that helped a little, at least protecting them from the dust which bit into his unprotected neck and face like little slivers of glass.

But Stone suddenly had a lot more to worry about than some heavy-duty razor cuts—he saw it, even through the curtains of sand, coming in from the west. It was huge, a funnel of wind, of black churning energy a good half mile wide. It seemed to extend high into the cloud line piercing them like some sort of Indian rope trick. And even from a few miles off he could hear the sound it made above the whistling sand. Stone didn't like the sound one bit, the grinding and crunching as everything the tornado passed over was being ripped up and systematically dismantled like it was all made of toothpicks.

He could feel the sheer energy of the thing, like one can sense the power of a great fighter as he walks by. It moved slowly with a kind of arrogance. The towering black chimney seemed to change direction almost at will as if it were curious about certain features in the landscape or wanted to go tear up a forest of low trees and send them flying into the air, twisted trunks and broken branches. And just as Stone thought he might actually get by it through a series of narrow plateaus as the land dropped lower out of the Colorado highlands descending into northern Texas and the great ranges, the tornado suddenly shifted right toward him and chugged with the roar of an H-bomb.

It's an interesting experience having a mile-high funnel of megadeath coming straight at you like it wants to shake your hand—off your body. And Stone wasn't all that interested in making the acquaintance with the death spiral. He veered the bike to the right and floored it, taking his chances that a gust of wind would knock him over. He got the Harley up to about thirty, letting both booted feet slam down every few seconds to keep balance and sending up clouds of dust along each side of the bike's trail. Stone's very bones felt like they were being shaken inside a blender.

It seemed like it was going to work—at first. Then the tornado veered again as if it had eyes in its dark head and knew what it wanted. And it came straight toward him.

"Give me a fucking break," the receiver of unwanted attentions screamed up at the black skies, wondering if the very gods had it in for him, because it sure as hell seemed that way. He hadn't said his prayers for quite a while. That was it. "I pray dear God—save my ass," Stone screamed into the wind, but not even his own ears could hear above the roar of the approaching funnel. It was as if he were standing at the edge of the main runway at the largest airport in the world and a thousand jets were all revving their engines at once. Stone wanted to throw his hands over his ears as the noise hurt his eardrums, made them feel like they were thinking of snapping like the skins of an old drumhead. But as his fingers were holding the handlebars of his bike it didn't seem like the greatest idea.

The entire landscape to his west was now taken up by the swirling funnel, and Stone could see into it now, could see the multicurrents of inner motion, a thousand complex interactions of wind all buffeting one another and moving in concentric circles within it. And it was filled, like the vacuum cleaner that it was, with everything it had passed over. Trees, animals, birds, grass, bush and thousands of tons of dirt all revolved within like the filthy clothes of an entire city in some gigantic washing machine in the sky. And even as Stone ripped back on the accelerator trying to make a final dash out of harm's way, he knew he wasn't going to make it.

Suddenly it was upon him, and it was as if he were in a dream. The entire bike was lifted into the air as the sheer wall of blackness closed right over him. There was no sky, no world, no nothing except the spinning end over end, not knowing where or who he was. He could feel the sheer energy of the thing as he entered its very fabric. He could feel the moisture of the funnel, the roaring crushing power of its 400 mph-plus winds which swung him around its outer edge. And he could feel as well the sheer malevolence of the thing, like it had a consciousness and it was to destroy.

Stone saw an entire tree coming toward him like it was playing a game of chicken. At the last possible second the thing suddenly shot up out of his way as though it had been hooked by a fisherman in the clouds. But something tore into the side of Stone's head, for he felt himself stunned and a sharp pain rip through his right temple. He squeezed his hands instinctively around the bars and wrapped his legs tighter against the sides as he struggled to hang onto consciousness. Now he was going even faster and he could dimly see the outer world, the trees, the prairie spinning as though he were on a turntable, as things pulled up from the sundered earth below shot by all around him.

Stone suddenly knew he'd be seeing his mother and father again real soon. Well, that would be nice. He wondered in a strangely calm way within the storm of his fear just what it would be like to die. And suddenly he wished with a burst of incredible force that surged through his body right up from the depths of his libido that he could get laid once more before he died.

CHAPTER
Three

WHEN Stone came to he was lying in the middle of what looked like one of the major battles of World War II. Dead, broken, twisted things lay everywhere. Trees had been ripped from the ground, their roots trailing behind like tendrils dripping green blood. The animal life had been decimated as if Mother Nature had come to hate all that she had created and wanted to kick some bloody booty. Fur, legs, grisly blood-soaked things not even recognizable anymore lay strewn everywhere amidst the carnage. Even the soil itself had not been spared as great chunks of it had been ripped up, the surface of the terrain gouged out in many spots for yards down, taking all the topsoil, the nutrients away so that the tornado's legacy would last far beyond the damage it had created today.

As Stone's head cleared slightly he suddenly realized he was sitting on dirt. Excaliber? The bike? He turned his head this way and that and nearly screamed out with pain as he felt that his neck was stiff as a board. Every other part of him wasn't doing great, he discovered, as he rose up and immediately fell back down again. His joints, muscles, and one knee all felt like they had been through a wrestling match with a grizzly. He must have taken some fall from that merry-go-round from hell. He walked a few steps and nearly stumbled on the crushed head and shoulders of an elk that had been torn raggedly in two. Stone looked around, reaching down for a branch which he used to support himself and his aching right leg. Then he did a quick walkabout of the nearby area searching for bike and dog.

The devastation was so intense it was as if an atomic bomb had gone off. The landscape had been made to look almost like the moon because where the trees had been ripped free of their moorings, huge holes were left, and craters gouged right out of the soil. It was ugly, as if the earth had been raped. Stone had read about the power of tornados but had never really given too much credence to it all. How the sheer force, the velocity of the swirling winds could generate such speed and power that straws could be driven through inch thick metal. He didn't see that straw —but he did see a branch that had been driven right into the side of a boulder, about five feet of it was still protruding out at about a forty five degree angle. The leaves had all been stripped off but it was clear that the rest of the branch had penetrated cleanly inside the granite boulder a good ten feet in diameter. It looked surreal, like something Picasso might have created on a particularly rambunctious night. Doubtless it would have brought huge bucks in the SoHo art world. When there had been such things.

Where the hell was the dog? He began fearing the worst —that he might well never see the animal again, alive or dead, or the Harley. That they'd just been swept off like Dorothy in the *Wizard of Oz* and were now in another state, crushed into a stew of dog and twisted motorcycle parts. He kept trying to wipe the image from his mind, but just as quickly it kept reasserting itself like a bad dream that wouldn't go away. Stone began feeling sick in the very pit of his stomach.

He walked through the rubble for nearly an hour, making wider and wider circles, poking through the debris, the overturned trees with his stick. Everything was in such shambles it was hard to even see clearly, like a forest that had been turned on its head, and sprinkled liberally with

dirt. At last, his lips grim as pencil lines, his throat tight-
ening up so he could hardly breathe, Stone sat down
against the trunk of a fallen tree and let out a long sigh. It
was all gone, the animal was dead. He threw his head back
to look up at the sky, wanting to make contact for a few
seconds perhaps, with a God he wasn't sure he even believed in. And then he let out a strange sound, a mix of
disbelief and joy.

About twenty-five feet up, nestled in one of the trees
that hadn't been taken down, was the bike, and it looked
like the box that the canine had been in was still attached to
the back, though he couldn't see inside it from where he
was. A smile spread across Stone's face and he felt the
pain in his entire body subside to about a tenth of what it
had been. It wasn't total disaster time yet. Within seconds
the smile began fading as he realized the bike was twenty-
five feet up in the air, lodged in the side of a tree like it was
planning on building a nest there. Slight problem. No big
deal, he'd just call in Rent-A-Crane.

Stone walked over to the ninth wonder of the world and
around the base of the tree a few times. It was easy to see
why the tornado hadn't gotten this baby. It was thick as a
sequoia and had branches that you could have constructed a
house on. The sides of the bark were peppered with little
dots and Stone looked close, seeing small bits of gravel
embedded in them. The force of the funnel had sent bits of
rock shrapnel flying out everywhere. That accounted for
the little blood blisters all along his exposed flesh. He was
lucky it hadn't been worse.

The branches of the tree looked like they formed a kind
of handhold path to the bike. The problem was getting up
the first eight feet or so. He found a foothold on a protruding knob and pushed up hard, jumping up with his arms at
the same time. Stone barely caught hold around the next
branch and swung there for a few seconds, his hands clawing at the hard, almost reptilian textured bark. Then realizing he was about to fall backwards he somehow sent out a
little extra and scampered aboard the thing, kicking and

grabbing at it like a wildman. Once on, it wasn't too hard to climb to the next and then up. Within a minute he was alongside the bike.

He came up to the back box, his heart beating fast, and could hardly bring himself to peer over. For if the dog wasn't inside, then. . . . But he saw fur as he pulled himself slowly up to the level of the black box. The dog was inside. He had strapped the canine down tightly enough to hold it in one place. At the time it had seemed like he was overdoing the whole thing with double cables everywhere. But it had unquestionably meant the dog's life. Stone found a hold along the back of the bike and sat between the two joining branches. He reached out and stroked the animal's side, feeling for heartbeat and breath. At first he felt nothing, but the pit bull was still warm though his lungs weren't moving as far as he could tell. But as he held his hand right over the ribcage he felt it, a dim but unwavering beat. Although somebody up there sure as hell seemed to have it in for Martin Stone, the same party or parties sure as hell seemed to favor the pit bull. If it had nine lives—it had just used up about half of them.

"Great!" Stone muttered as his mood grew dark again, from a pure hit of relief into a funk within a few seconds. The road to manic depression. Now he just had to get everybody down. He looked down. It was impossible. Perhaps he could get the dog, but. . . . "Shit," he snapped at himself; he knew he was going to have to try. He climbed up a notch and opened another box alongside the dog's. Inside were supplies he had filled the Harley with before leaving the bunker, the retreat, dug into the side of a mountain that his father, Col. Clayton Stone, had built years before. Thank God he had included ropes in the box. As he had to spend some time in the mountains recently— and it had been without weapons or ropes—he had overcompensated for this trip. The cable he'd taken was the best he found in the supply room of the bunker. Half inch wrapped nylon, tested to hold over a ton. And a pulley system. That wasn't tested nearly so high. But Stone wasn't going to worry about that right now.

He got the whole pulley/cable system rigged up, attaching the holding end to a branch about six feet above the bike. He let the ropes fall to the ground and then swung out on the thing testing it. Strong as a ship cable. Stone lowered himself via his hand all the way down to the ground, and then hoisted himself back up checking for any snags. But the system, an ultra-expensive mountain scaling outfit, appeared to work perfectly. Stone undid the entire box that the dog was in and snapped clamps around the four steel rings on it. Then setting his feet against a branch he let the animal down real slow. The block and tackle was gear-ratioed so that it was fairly easy to handle, the weight feeling like only about twenty or thirty pounds of pressure on the ropes he was releasing inches at a time. The box hit the ground softly and Stone released his end and again swung down.

He hit the ground on his uninjured leg and pulled the box a safe distance away from the tree. He undid the dog's bindings within the box just in case he didn't come out alive from what he was about to attempt. And if he did get crushed by the huge Harley he didn't want to leave the dog tied up, unable to defend itself, not that it was moving too swiftly. Just in case something came looking for food.

"I'm such a fucking optimist, that's what I like about myself," Stone commented dryly as he stood up from the dog, motionless as a stuffed animal, lips pulled back to reveal the long sharp canines, which protruded down as if wishing they could sink into something thick and meaty.

"Take it easy pal, in case we don't get to talk again," Stone said and then walked back to the tree like he was walking down the final corridor to the execution chamber. He didn't have a good feeling about it at all. The dog was one thing but the bike—it weighed—he couldn't even imagine. Perhaps a ton with all the excess gear he had stashed around the thing. Stone realized this was going to be a longer operation than he had envisioned. He'd have to strip the entire bike if he had the slightest chance of getting it down from its lofty heights. Cursing under his breath at the incredible hassle that lay ahead, Stone took out his pliers and wrenches and undid every single box and weapon on the bike, including the Luchaire 89mm missile system that he had put on only a week before. He hooked them up to the pulley, then lowered each one slowly down. He then lowered himself, moved the excess baggage away from the tree so the next load could be sent down, and climbed back up again.

It took five hours to get the bike completely stripped but at last Stone was looking at the last and the only trip that mattered—the Harley itself. He clipped the six hooks in what seemed like a symmetrical arrangement around the bike. It was hard to tell just how the weight should be distributed, but he did his best. His main concern was not so much whether the cables held—according to his calculations they should, but whether he could handle the weight of it, even with the six-to-one weight ratio of the pulley system, and even with a rope wrapped around a branch that he could release bit by careful bit.

Looking up and seeing the slight color of the late afternoon darkening behind far forests that had survived the tornado's onslaught, Stone knew he had to move fast. In the darkness it would be a joke.

He set his legs as firmly as he could between two branches so he was wedged in and pulled up with everything he had. Slowly, inch by agonizing inch, he got the Harley to lift up from its resting place between the two branches. He knew instantly that he'd taken on much more than he'd bargained for. Every fraction of an inch was almost impossible. There was no way in hell he'd make it all the way to the ground. When the bike had lifted above the branch edge so it appeared to have clearance, Stone let out a yell and turned his body to the side so the entire pulley swiveled above him. The branch it was attached to wasn't about to give, it was three feet thick at the base where the cable was attached. But the cable itself was stretching and making sharp sounds like something under incredibly high tension, giving off high harmonic overtones.

Stone started to lower the bike, feeling his hands turning red and ripped from holding the rope. It started its descent inch by inch dangling around in the air as it twisted back and forth. And it was the turning motion that caused the problem, for suddenly as it reached its outer swing one of the clips ripped free, unable to take the extra weight. As the bike swung back to the other side, another clip went. And that was that. Suddenly they all ripped free and the weight on the rope Stone was holding went to zero like a fishing line that a fish had just bid adieu. He watched with horror as the bike dropped straight down.

CHAPTER
Four

IT was too late to see if the Harley was still functional, and Stone was too tired to try. He set up the machine gun from the bike on the dirt, built a small fire a few yards from it and sat there on his bedding morosely eating a can of Spam, with the dog lying in the metal box alongside him. He sat for hours staring into the flame-licked darkness and swore he kept seeing things, shadows of things darting everywhere. And sounds. But at last he fell asleep in spite of himself, both hands fastened tightly around the machine gun like he was holding a baby.

When Stone awoke it was with a start. Something was in front of him—and it had teeth. And when his hands pulled back instinctively on the twin triggers the sound of the machine gun letting loose with a twenty-shot volley made his eyes open wide and fast. It took him a few seconds to even realize it was he who had fired the burst and he looked around frantically searching for the enemy upon him. But all he could see was the backside of a groundhog which he had scared the living shit out of and was hightailing its way back under some fallen trees, its fur bristling everywhere.

Once he realized just what had transpired Stone's mouth grew into a smile, then a laugh, then a whole gale of laughter that burst from him in an avalanche of pain and anxiety suddenly released. So he was reduced to taking out groundhogs with a .50-caliber. He pulled his hands away from the smoking gun and stood up. He hadn't slept well at all and already was getting a throbbing headache from the noise. He dropped down on one knee and stirred around the embers of the fire. The thing was still going; with a few branches thrown on, the flames quickly sprang back up to life. Stone took out a small pot from one of the boxes he had taken off the Harley's back mounted rack and walked about fifty yards before he came to a small stream that trickled slowly by. The water smelled good. He leaned down and took a lick from a palmful. Tasted good too.

Stone filled the pot and his canteen and headed back. He threw some instant coffee into the scratched-up pot and placed it down on top of the now crackling fire. The brew was bitter, for the instant coffee was years old, from the bunker's supply stores. But still it was coffee and had that jolt he needed to click his body and brain into gear. He started a second cup and was at last able to look over at the bike, completely disassembled with its component parts lying around it.

The first thing to check out was the Harley itself. It seemed impossible that it hadn't suffered major damage in the fall. Stone sat on top of the thing and rocked it around beneath his legs. The bike seemed solid enough. The wheels looked aligned, the bars, everything. It appeared to have been able to withstand the shock. He tried the ignition and the motorcycle started up with a lion roar and then settled quickly back into a growl. He kept it in neutral and gave it some gas and the motor seemed to be all right. He got off, double-checked both tires making sure they were tightened, and then went on with the job of loading everything back again.

Once he actually got going Stone found it wasn't that bad. Since he had already put the thing together and taken it apart now he didn't waste a lot of time figuring out angles and clasps. Lost in concentration as he reattached every part, he didn't even realize he was done until he looked around and there was nothing more to reattach. Stone stood up and looked at his creation. Not bad. The Luchaire 89mm firing tube looked a trifle lopsided as it sat attached to the left side of the bike. He readjusted it.

"Not bad, not fucking bad, heh dog?," Stone commented, glancing over at the pit bull which was lying in its little mobile casket. Stone was so used to making snide comments to the animal, he had forgotten it was not in a hearing state of mind. He clamped his lips shut like he wasn't going to say another word this year and mounted the dirt-covered Harley. He started her up and headed slowly ahead, keeping both feet flat on the ground, as he wouldn't have been surprised to find the thing cracking right in half after the fall it had taken. But other than a few new creaks and groans here and there as the metal moved around a little readjusting itself, everything seemed like it was going to stay in one place.

Within minutes he was moving at about forty, and for the first time that morning he relaxed a little, realizing as he did just how uptight he must have been. His stomach let loose with a whole rush of gurgles as the muscles within unclenched. Now, all he needed was to find the nearest McDonald's, or the post-nuke version of such anyway, which meant a rabbit on the hoof.

Stone realized that other than the Spam and a few pieces of candy bar he had choked down with coffee, he had hardly eaten a thing for days now. It was hard to grab a bite sometimes when the whole world was trying to kill you.

Either he hadn't noticed them before, because he had been so busy in his repair work, or else there hadn't been as many where he and the dog had been spat out by the tornado—but suddenly Stone noticed a shitload of birds. He saw vultures as he focused in on a few of them munching on carcasses around the open prairie he was cruising down. With all the carrion around—and he could smell it in the air now, the heavy scent of rotting meat—the decay eaters were having a field day.

Vultures were everywhere. The bent ugly heads were

ripping into their meals in loud snapping groups on every side. Stone raised his eyes up and nearly gasped, for the sky above, relatively clear after the squalls of yesterday, was brimming with the creatures. Stone had never seen so many of the wide-winged birds. They seemed to fill the whole sky, flying in an immense circle that must have stretched out for a mile. There had to be thousands of them all flapping wildly as they went faster and faster and dropped lower. Stone had seen vultures eating before. But they were always in much smaller groups, perhaps a few dozen around a dead buffalo. This was of a vastly different order.

It wasn't just the numbers that started getting him a little nervous as he rode through the destruction and the countless feasts of their huge groups—it was their attitude. They were getting frenzied, wild, making screaming sounds constantly and flapping their wings. In some carrion gluts they were ripping into each other, not out of protecting their food, it appeared, but out of sheer madness as they began plucking at each other with sharp hooked beaks that could tear through the thickest of hides. Their frenzy reminded Stone of films he'd seen on the feeding frenzies of sharks when they gathered in large groups around a kill, a whale or something big. They would start hitting at anything, each other, even themselves.

But he didn't think birds were supposed to act that way. Yet these were. Swooping in great herds of dark feathers, the vultures built larger and larger circles in the sky as other carrion eaters gathered from hundreds of miles around to take part in the smorgasbord of decay. He could see the whole situation was going to explode. There were just too many bumping into each other until the very heavens seemed filled with nothing but feathers. Stone knew something was going to go. It was like a supersaturated chemical—with the addition of just another drop, it goes over the edge and crystallizes. Only when these birds went it wasn't into crystals but virulent madness.

Suddenly they were diving down like kamikaze bombers

slamming into others of their species and any other unfortunate living things below. Beaks slashed and snapped at everything, even trees and rocks. They bit into one another in the air and on the ground with vicious snaps. This was no fun and games, but ten thousand six-foot-wingspanned birds who had all gone bananas. And Stone just happened to be in the same madhouse.

Suddenly there was a loud snapping of wings just above him and he tipped his head up to see about a dozen of the gangly creatures coming down like misfired missiles. Stone swerved the Harley to the right at the same instant he ripped out his 9mm Beretta. He sprayed the thing above and around him in the air and saw feathers and blood go flying in all directions as a few of them plummeted to the ground behind him. But it was as if they knew no fear, they were beyond all that. It was a frenzy of pure numbers, of losing what little mind a vulture has and letting it all go in a kind of bacchanalian feast to the gods, a blood-drunken orgy from which many would not emerge alive.

Stone suddenly let the bike rip forward, wanting to just get the hell out of there and fast. He accelerated to fifty miles per hour, not wanting to go much faster as the long stretch of prairie was marred with holes and ridges. And if he went down in the midst of all this. . . . Stone didn't let his mind dwell on it.

A dead wild bull that had been decapitated by the tornado was lying about forty yards off to the right, and a virtual blanket of feathers covered the thing, ripping it like there was no tomorrow. Usually vultures were attracted to the motionless, the still, the dead. But their excitement had altered their behavior patterns—and it was Stone's bike that suddenly caught their attention as he tore past.

There was a thunderous flapping of wings that totally unnerved Stone. When he swung his head around not slowing an inch he saw every feathery son-of-a-bitching one of them rising up en masse. They were not exactly graceful birds and slammed and bumped into each other all over the place, actually knocking each other out in some cases so that limp wings spiraled down to the ground where they lay broken. But the rest, several hundred of them, rose up about eighty feet, circling the bull a few times just to get their bearings, and then took chase after one Martin Stone.

Stone couldn't believe it as he kept glancing over his shoulder, and the flock kept growing closer by the second. They were clearly coming after him, doubtless already salivating or drooling whatever juices flowed in a vulture's beak. Stone swung the autopistol back over his shoulder without even looking, just gauging the angle of fire, and pulled. He held the trigger until the clip was emptied, and then snapped a quick look around. A whole slew of them were plummeting down and a few were also dropping behind to eat them. But in general it hadn't done a hell of a lot of good. In fact, unless Stone's eyes were deceiving him, more seemed to be joining in the chase as the entire circle of vultures which had been flying far above like a beacon to other carrion eaters throughout the state also started dropping fast. Oh, he'd definitely caught their attention.

Like an oasis in the middle of a desert Stone saw a thicket of low trees ahead and a sort of pathway leading into them. It looked passable, for him anyway. He leaned forward on the bike and tore into it, slowing the Harley as soon as he hit the path to make sure he could effect passage. He could. Stone heard a fluttering right above the tree canopy. Some of the foolhardy creatures were landing on the interwoven branches above. They were obviously intent on getting to him, no ifs, ands or buts about it, though just what it was that made him so fucking attractive to them was a question Stone was burning to know. Maybe it was the dog lying on the back. He looked dead. Maybe it was as if he were toying with them, dangling a mouse in front of a cat and then running with it. Well, these suckers had gone for the bait.

Stone debated staying inside the thicket but after a few seconds of listening to their frantic attempts to break down and through the branches he decided against it. He started ahead switching on the lights to navigate through the shadows of the mini-jungle of trees and bush. The pathway that appeared man-made extended right through the thicket. Stone found a comfortable speed and moved along at about twenty, his boots digging down in the black soil. He no longer heard the flutterings and the smashings of beaks and talons against wood, and breathed a sigh of relief. He'd lost them. That was the one saving grace about vultures—they were stupid.

After about five minutes Stone saw light ahead and suddenly broke through a few vines dangling down over his face, slicing along his chin. He was out into the dimness of the end of day. Only as he emerged he saw that something was blotting out the sinking sun ahead. And as he adjusted to the light Stone saw that the sky ahead was filled with an army of them, a single immense circle which turned with thousands upon thousands of birds. As thick and as awe-inspiring as the very rings of Saturn, only this ring was of leathery hide and dark feathers. And it was after him.

The circle that hovered about five hundred feet above the terrain began dropping the moment he emerged from the grove. Stone knew it was too late to even try to turn around and get back. They'd be on him before he was halfway there. He could only move ahead. He slammed his finger on the firing button of the 50-cal mounted on the front of the bike, swiveling it so it was arched up at a forty-five degree angle pointing straight into the descending flock. Then he pushed hard and held the button down as the barrel burped out a fusillade of thick finger-sized slugs. The whole bottom part of the descending horde seemed to disintegrate before his eyes, as hundreds of the crank-necked buzzards flopped to the ground wings broken, heads hanging limply to one side.

They retreated momentarily, swooping up and then turned far around, taking almost a mile to do so. But then they started back again, this time gaining speed from far off. It was as if they were going to come down on him with

the sheer kinetic motion of their bodies, let him try to shoot
them down or not as he wished. Stone gulped hard. The
50-cal wasn't going to do it. They were ready to die—or
didn't know the meaning of it.

Suddenly he remembered the Luchaire. He had attached
this one as opposed to the first launcher he had had, which
had been lost along with his Harley Electraglide in an avalanche. This one had a swivel mount so it could be pulled
out and fired on the move. Now was as good as any for a
try. Stone pulled his leg up and out of the way and un-
hitched the firing tube. There was no time for careful cal-
culation, but he quickly tilted it up directly toward the
center of the sky armada. There was time for only one
shot, he had to stop to reload—and that didn't seem too
likely.

Don't fire until you see the whites of their eyes. The
words tore through his mind like an advertising ditty. Only
these suckers didn't have whites in their eyes—besides,
they were already too close; Stone could see the crooked
beaks snapping in the air, the cold predatory eyes beaming
in on him, preparing to make contact the hard way. He
lifted his leg back so he was riding at a peculiar angle and
pulled the trigger. The whole bike shook with a roar as the
missile shot out the tube, and a blue flame exhaust, the
heat of which Stone could feel like a blast furnace, shot
past him on the side of the seat.

But it was the missile end that was the thing to look out
for. And the vultures didn't have a chance. The 89mm
shell set to detonate at the lightest contact ripped through
the first few ranks of the garbage birds about a hundred
yards away and went in a good two hundred feet before it
found something hard enough to go off of. And it went
with an immense explosion which Stone wasn't quite prepared for, nearly knocking the bike over on its side. The
force of the blast tore out in every direction into the vultures, absolutely ripping them to shreds. It was like a
chicken butchering factory run by anarchists, for the vultures were sliced up into all sorts of odd configurations,

few of them marketable. Wings, beaks, claws all went shooting off in every direction as the whole sky filled with feathers and a mist of blood that colored the high clouds scarlet.

Stone withstood the initial shock blast and pulled his goggles down as he tore on straight ahead and into the mess. The blood mist was dropping now and the feathers too so that there was a storm of them. He could hardly see and had to slow down to almost nothing before he at last emerged on the other side and was clear of the falling storm of fluffy red soaked feathers.

There were no more of them waiting for him. It didn't make him feel great to see so much bloodshed, so many butchered vultures. But what went around came around, and these buzzards had learned the hard way. Stone drove on just as other flocks of them began circling again. But this time their attention was zeroed in on their dead brethren below. It made the other isolated bits of carrion as much as there was like a mere snack compared to the acres of pulverized and homogenized bird flesh. Within minutes of his departure from the killing ground Stone could see the new cloud forming above the serve-yourself vulture meat market like some vast swirling asteroid belt of brown bodies. And as he drove over a rise and didn't look back again, the blood flock dropped down like a curtain descending.

CHAPTER
Five

A young woman stood naked on a pedestal. The pedestal, electronically controlled, was revolving as greedy eyes took in the nubile lithe form, untouched, unscarred and untwisted by life, unlike those faces that stared at it.

"Beautiful, so beautiful," the Dwarf said from his wheelchair as he tried to rise up on his stumps to his full height like a bird trying to present its plumage. Only he didn't have any plumage to present.

"Yes," other voices spoke from around the stainless steel floor. They stared hard at her perfect beauty contrasting so starkly with their own physical abnormalities. The dozen people in the room, the Dwarf's personal staff, were also freaks—three men who were badly burned, other dwarfs, a man with no flesh, only pulsing muscle visible to all the world. These were the Dwarf's own, the ones he felt comfortable with within his private twenty thousand square foot chamber deep in the NAUASC underground quarters.

"She shall look so beautiful for the wedding," a female midget with a face twisted up like a Mack truck had run over it a few times, said from one side of the slowly turning woman. She was hardly more than in her late teens and her eyes weren't really focused on anything. But her mouth was set in terror as if her face knew she was scared shitless, even though her brain was numbed out by several drugs that the Dwarf had injected into her.

"Yes, the wedding," other voices repeated beneath the overly bright lights of the chamber.

"Oh thank you all for your compliments," the Dwarf said, bowing from side to side from his wheelchair. "For I too am delighted by my imminent wedding. And by the beauty of my blushing bride." Blushing was hardly the word for it. The girl's face was flushed like she'd been in the sun all day long from the drugs she was on, a side effect of the mind-altering chemicals.

"Now we must complete the bridal gown design," the female dwarf said, squealing as she hopped around on the floor reaching out to touch the naked girl, whose hands were over her pubic area, shy even in a state of near mind-lessness.

"Yes, begin the fitting," the Dwarf squealed in a high-pitched voice, and the place erupted in merriment. Materials and scissors were brought out and all kinds of fitting and cutting of fabrics went on for an hour as the Dwarf looked on with a most contented smile across his pushed-in face. At last the white satin dress and trim were all tucked into place with pins and needles and the girl's hair was pulled back and done up into the style the Dwarf liked— one he had chosen after looking through a number of old bridal magazines. It was his first and only marriage. He wanted things to go—so nicely. And for his bride to look her most beautiful.

"Yes, yes, it is excellent," the Dwarf laughed, slamming his stumps against one another so they thwacked together with fleshy sounds right in front of his face. "And now the rose, the black rose—bring it out." A three-armed man walked solemnly out holding a golden tray. With one hand holding the tray, and one raising the cover, the third hand lifted a black rose and reached out and pinned it to April's shoulder. It was black as midnight, black as oil that had slept in the very center of the earth. It looked, to the

Dwarf's and the rest of the assemblage's eyes anyway, so lovely against the virgin white of the bridal gown.

"Yes, she is a picture of my divine dream," Dwarf said softly. For the Dwarf had had a dream years before of his bride-to-be. The woman who would someday bear his children to carry on with the empire that he was creating. A son who would rule the world. And she would be the mother of the thing, of the monster that the Dwarf knew would surely emerge.

"Come to me my lovely," he said, sitting back in the wheelchair, as a dark smile flickered back and forth across his mouth. She was led slowly over by two elephant-faced twins to the Dwarf until she stood just a few inches away and was level with the misshapen handless and legless monstrosity standing up on his stumps in the chair. He looked deep into her eyes like he was searching for something.

"Do not be afraid my child," the Dwarf said softly. "No harm shall come to you."

"I am afraid," she replied so softly it was hard to hear. But he had heard.

"No, no," the Dwarf laughed. "You will see, my precious. You will be rich and powerful beyond all dreams. Being the wife of the Dwarf shall make you the most powerful woman on the planet. Together we shall rule, you shall bear my children." Even in the midst of her drug-induced half trance, the words seemed to do something to April, for she looked like she was going to puke suddenly and her face turned as white as a freshly laundered sheet.

"Your—children?" she whispered. "Oh my God." Her mouth opened to scream but instead she just sort of wobbled around in place like she was thinking of going into the land of Nod from the sheer thought.

"Come to me my precious," the Dwarf said again, spreading his stumps for her to approach. "Come to me." He stared deep into her eyes and she was unable to pull her gaze away. She was in a deep fog, as if on the bottom of the ocean and everything was black all around her. Only his eyes seemed real. They told her what to do.

"Yes, that's it, bring your face to me," the Dwarf commanded soothingly. "Now kiss me. Kiss these lips." He pursed his lips and the gold capped teeth within shone in the center of the egg-shaped face. She brought her face closer to the little hideousness but she felt her guts rising up at every fraction of an inch. Then her lips were against his and he moved his gold teeth against her so they felt cold. And then a thin reptilian tongue, squirming like a worm and cold, unearthly cold, slid into her mouth and seemed to try to wrap around her tongue.

Suddenly April's mouth flew open and a geyser of vomit spewed up into the air as she flew back and away from the outstretched stumps. A spray of the stuff landed on the Dwarf's face and shoulders as she collapsed onto the floor, her overloaded nervous system unable to cope with the love affair. The Dwarf stared down at her, his face a mass of quivering rage as underlings rushed forward and dabbed at the puke with wet cloths. He was ready to kill but pushed it down as he didn't want even those "closest" to him to see. He especially didn't want them to see. He laughed loud and shrill, setting even the dullest of ears on edge.

"She loves me so. Ah, she is overcome with emotion and tenderness. Ours will indeed be a fruitful union. Take her things to be sewn, we will move on with the wedding plans at full speed," the Dwarf commanded his lackeys. They quickly dressed April, putting a loose fitting pajama-type outfit they had been marching her around in for the last week since the Dwarf had taken her prisoner and become engaged to her all in one fell swoop.

"Give her more drugs," he whispered, gritting his capped teeth. "She needs more."

"Yes, Great One," the three-armed man replied, saluting with all three arms at once. "More drugs. We shall bring love to her heart through the molecule, not the myth."

"What is the union of pure blackness and perfect light?" the Dwarf asked the three-armed man.

"Gray, excellency, it can only be," the three-armed servant replied, bowing slightly as no one could look him directly in the eye. Not that anyone wanted to.

"No, it is a blackness that can absorb the rainbow. A blackness with the qualities of white. A master color, Skarnoff. A color above all other colors capable of absorbing all of them as well. A ruling color, Skarnoff."

"Yes excellency, I understand."

"Yes, I'm sure," the Dwarf laughed. He needed Skarnoff for he was the most intelligent among the Dwarf's underlings, and feared him as well, for he was immensely powerful. And fear was not permissible in the Dwarf's world. Yet he didn't wish to kill him, for the man had been loyal and obedient. He had helped the Dwarf kill many men and would doubtless kill more. As long as the man didn't flinch when Dwarf looked at him, didn't betray the slightest aura of traitorousness, he would let him live. And the Dwarf could tell when they were lying. He could always tell.

"But now," Dwarf said, slamming his left stump into the panel of the chair so it swiveled around and headed toward a large list that had been spread out on a table. He came to a stop in front of the thing and rose up on his stumps leaning forward.

"Yes, meats, wines, fruits, drugs—all is here, excellent, excellent." Suddenly his eyes froze on one of the pages.

"What's this here?" he asked, his voice rising. "There are no doves here to release as I requested. In my dream, there were always doves. There must be, you hear me," the Dwarf was shrieking now at full pitch, his thin veneer of patience gone. "If you have to catch pigeons and paint them white do it and don't tell me, but there'd better be some fucking white doves at my wedding—or your heads will have feathers glued onto them and be thrown into the air." The dove procurers went fleeing from the chamber like they were running from the devil himself.

CHAPTER

Six

DRIVING nonstop through the night Stone figured he made a few hundred miles which wasn't bad considering. He hopped a few back country roads, but couldn't hook into anything big or that lasted for very long. Most of the time it was over bumpy and fissured prairie land which seemed to stretch off forever. It was just nearing dawn, the sky starting to turn an ocean blue, when he saw a sign toppled to one side of the two-laner he had found and been cruising for an hour.

"WELCOME TO THE LONE STAR STATE OF TEXAS." And something else greeted him within minutes as he drove on into the state of giant everything—giant craters standing on each side of the road like an apocalyptic welcoming committee. Stone shuddered, he hated the damn things, not least because there was no way of knowing whether or not they were still radioactive. That was the thing about the stuff—it was invisible, yet could kill you as surely as a bullet or a knife, only worse. Still, these were far enough off the road, each at least two miles away, so that Stone figured he'd just move fast through it all and hope for the best.

But within another ten minutes of driving he saw that there were craters dotting the whole landscape. This part of northwest Texas looked like it had been hit with a fucking

barrage of the things. Stone knew there were air force
bases out here, and other military complexes. But it looked
like overkill to say the least. As he scanned the land in the
light of the hesitantly arriving dawn he could count ten of
them within his range of vision in all directions of the
compass. Maybe someone had the bright idea of setting the
oil fields of Texas on fire. All of them—and sending the
whole damn state up in a blast of black smoke that would
have been visible from the moon. But though they had
bombed the shit out of everything in sight, no super oil fire
seemed to have erupted.

Stone drove on, keeping on the road because it gave him
much better time than the bumpy wastelands. But he grew
increasingly nervous about the craters as another one just
ahead seemed to come almost up alongside the two-laner.
He slowed down as he rounded a bend and saw the thou-
sand-foot-high mound of rock and dirt like something from
the dark side of the moon sitting just ahead about five
hundred yards from the road. It towered over the roadway
impossibly big and thick, and clearly man-made, for nature
in her worst disasters never made things that looked quite
like this, filled with an aura of death, the scent of it riding
on the wind.

It was with disbelieving eyes that Stone saw a shack
built just off the side of the road, right beneath the shadow
of the great crater. He slowed the bike down and looked
with even more amazement when he saw that people lived
there, kids and dogs jumping around in front of the place.
And a big sign hung lopsided up on the caved-in roof.

"SAM'S STORE." And beneath that in smaller letters,
apparently the store's motto: "You want it—we ain't got
it." He pulled into the place, figuring he could afford a
minute or two in the proximity of the crater to see what the
hell was going on. Stone could see one thing instantly as
he drove in and put both feet down on the ground coming
to a full stop. The kids were dying. They had all kinds of
cancers growing on their skins, teeth missing, hair gone in
big clumps from their small heads, leaving bloody gouges

up top. Stone felt his Spam dinner rising up like a steer coming out of the gate. Even the dogs, running around like the playful animals they were, were missing huge clumps of hide, one had no ears, another a toothless mouth with oozing gums. How the hell could they all live this way? Didn't they understand the reasons for what was happening to them?

"Howdy mister," a voice said from out of the doorway of the shack and a figure walked out. It was a man about Stone's size who looked even more fucked up than the kids. He couldn't have weighed more than ninety pounds, and had sores covering every bit of his exposed flesh. Not a strand of hair remained on his head, just thousands of little red dots where hairs had once been. A single tooth remained in the middle of his mouth. Yet somehow the mouth was smiling and the man walking toward Stone acting as if everything was just fine.

"Need anything, stranger? We ain't got a hell of a lot in stock to be perfectly honest with you, that's why we got the sign." He grinned. "But what we do got ain't rotten, broken, or dying. And we got the best prices in the North Texas region. That I swear to you on a bible." Up close Stone could see the guy was completely falling apart. It was as if his very flesh was rotting at the seams, as if everything inside might just burst out some day pretty soon right now.

"Say, I know this is probably a dumb question," Stone said with a shy smile as he sat back on the bike, letting his hands fall from the bars, but keeping the engine running. "But did you ever notice that you were living right next door to an authentic atomic bomb crater? And that you— and your family—seem to have developed a few medical problems from it?"

"Oh heck, that," the man said, waving his hand at the crater like it was some old horse from the next county come to eat his garden. "Shoot, them things is all around these parts as far as a man can ride. These bumps and stuff," the man said, running his hands over his diseased flesh. "Everyone roun' here got em. That's just the way we all is now. Everyone."

"I see," Stone said numbly. What could he say? Or do. The world was far beyond his ability to influence more than a few micrometers' worth, if that. Who was he to even judge? These poor bastards had to adjust to what they had. And they had. So what if their lifespans were ten years or less. Or that their bodies were dripping swamps of ooze. People seemed able to get used to just about anything.

"So what kin I do you for mister? We got some good deals on cans of lima beans, three of them and not one rotted open yet. Got a jar of mustard—unopened," the man said proudly. "Got a can of genuine Budweiser beer. Was opened years ago, but we sealed it up again, you can still taste the original flavor. Whole can for a buck, a sip for a dime. We got—"

"Thanks," Stone said, shaking his head from side to side. "But I don't think so." The very thought of eating a single bite of the super-irradiated food, which had been soaking up God knew what for years now, was not something that Stone was about to pay money for. "Tell me, am I on the right road to Amarillo? I've got—some business there."

"Sure the hell are. Jes' keep going straight ahead 'bout thirty miles or so. Then you'll see this big ol' highway. It's busted up pretty bad in places, but with a cycle you could probably get through. Amarillo? Jeeez." The man seemed impressed by the idea. A mythical place far beyond anything he would ever reach again in his short moist life. "I was there once, can't even remember when now. But it was a big damned place, I remember that."

"Well listen," Stone said, revving up the bike. "You all take care now." He smiled at the kids who grinned shyly back. They were cute in a grisly sort of way beneath the sores and the flaking flesh and the cracked lips. Kids were kids, even when they were radioactive.

Stone could hardly bear to look at the entire assemblage

all staring at him. One of the dogs jumped up to be petted but tumbled back to the ground, hardly able to get up the energy. It fell over on its three working legs, the fourth a shriveled up little leathery thing, and squirmed around the ground pushing itself in a circle but unable to quite rise. Stone closed his eyes for a second and then opened them and started forward. He didn't look back.

As he drove along he saw others as well. The region was actually quite well-populated considering he hadn't seen a soul for about a hundred miles. And they all had the same radioactive afflictions covering their bodies. Shacks along the roadway were selling all sorts of things—foods, skins, artifacts from the past. And all of them were burnt and half destroyed—pelts hanging on a wall were actually burned through with holes in some places. Yet people were buying the stuff. To this crew it was all normal. A whole society based on the acceptance of radioactivity in everything, even themselves.

Stone wondered what happened to them when they died as he didn't see a single body lying around anywhere. With this bunch one would think death would be an hourly occurrence. But as he drove on past three more craters about five miles apart he came upon a line of several dozen of the dying. They were marching along slowly as if they had all the time in the world—which they didn't, seeing how they were rotting as they walked. These were even worse off than the ones he'd already passed, skin hanging off bone, faces dissolved down to the skeletal core. Drops of red and brown dripped from tears in their clothes, which were numerous. They had their arms atop the shoulders of the one in front of them like the blind leading the radioactive blind. And some clearly were without their sight anymore, with sockets filled with pink and black custard.

They took not the slightest heed of Stone as he drove slowly by them. The leader of the group looked the most diseased of all with no face whatsoever, just a mass of raw flesh and some holes where a mouth and nose and ears should be. Yet he led them forward with purpose, one shrunken leg slamming down, then the next. Stone gulped and turned away from the face which did not deign to look toward him. They were of two different worlds, heading in different directions.

Stone wondered just where the hell these guys were in such a mind to get to, but as he drove ahead about two miles he saw where they were going: to their burial ground. This was the field alongside the road where their ancestors had already marched the same trek. The dead fields on which not a thing grew were filled with bones and still-rotting corpses. There must have been hundreds of them, with their bones spread out for an acre or more. Some of the skeletons were in the shadows of the rocks that rose here and there, and Stone could see in the dimness that they glowed. The place must have been a sight at night, with all the remains glowing up a storm. A man could open an amusement park, or a restaurant across the road. The Eat By The Light of the Radioactive Dead Chow House. He wondered if he was cracking up.

It was getting dark but he didn't stick around to see the bone fireworks while heading south as fast as he dared travel in the twilight as the road grew steadily worse. He drove into the night, the Harley's headlight cutting through the blackness with a wide beam. Stone didn't stop until near midnight when he couldn't see a single one of the bomb craters, even standing on top of the bike and looking around 360 degrees. He made himself gulp down another can of Spam and some hard biscuits, then a handful of vitamins he had snatched from the bunker.

He camped out on a rise where he could see all around him nice and clear, and chewed down the lousy chow bite by unappetizing bite. The sight of all those rotting folks had done wonders for his stomach. But he knew if he didn't eat he'd start getting weak, even sick. This was not the way to travel around the new America. The weak perished as fast as they came along. They were the fodder of accelerating barbarism.

When he'd finished, Stone went over to the dog. It still

wasn't moving though the heart did not seem to have slowed since he'd last checked. He knew the animal hadn't eaten for days now. He made a gruel from some of the biscuits and some condensed milk, and then mixed it all together with water from his thermos to form a wet paste. Stone wedged the dog's mouth open and started slowly slopping small spoonfuls of the stuff in, then turned the animal's head from side to side trying to work some down. He spent nearly twenty minutes spooning the slop and could hardly even tell if any was getting down the canine's gullet, as much of it seemed to have fallen on Stone's pants and down to the ground. But with the very last spoonful the dog suddenly coughed and spat up a spray of the food, then lapsed right back into complete stillness.

Still it was movement of some kind. It showed the creature was still on this side of the black veil. Great, Stone thought darkly as he sat back against the bike, took out both of his pistols, and laid them on his lap for instant access. So the dog was alive. One fucking cough in three days and I think it's the medical miracle of the century. He somehow fell asleep but he slept fitfully, waking up and reaching for the guns as he thought he heard something. But each time it was just a dream, and he sank from one nightmare to another like a drowning man being bounced from wave to storming wave.

CHAPTER

Seven

THE next morning Stone woke to a biting rain, which had already soaked his hair and outer clothes. Thank God he'd covered Excaliber's box before he retired, or the deeply dreaming mutt would be floating in dog soup right now. He mounted up onto the bike, knowing it was too wet to even try to make a fire for coffee—and with all things considered—he was in just about the foulest mood he could remember, grayer even than the rain-streaked air around him, through which he could see but fifty or sixty feet. He stared straight ahead, grinding his teeth together with angry unconscious mouthings about the state of affairs. He then fell into a trance with all his attention on the road and its numerous holes and chasms already filling with water, some looking big enough for the bike to completely disappear into without a trace.

After about fifty miles Stone was slightly heartened to see a rusting sign that said Hartley was the next town. That meant Amarillo wasn't more than another thirty. He'd be there by nightfall. Not that he was greatly looking forward to it, since he had little or no idea of just how he was going to go about rescuing April. The Dwarf was the cleverest bastard he'd come up against and Stone knew he'd have to be extremely careful—and lucky—to come out of this one. He wished beyond measure that he'd killed the little bastard the last time they met—when he'd had the chance. If only he'd looked out the window and had seen that the murdering eggman had landed in water after his twelve-story fall. He could have torn ass downstairs and ended the threat to mankind with a few slugs. If, if, if. If a rat had a tux it would be a Senator. That's what his dad had always said. The Major hadn't gotten along with the political breed especially well.

With the rain continuing, the four-laner he was riding on became virtually unusable, and Stone had to take the next exit ramp, which was broken into jagged sections, though he was able to tear over it with a few quick jumps of the bike. Then he was back on sparsely bushed flat terrain with a few rolling hills to the east. He got up a good head of steam and headed south, keeping a close eye on the compass he'd super-glued to the top of the bike while in the bunker. The rain at last seemed to die out, though a constant irritating mist continued to fill the air, making him have to wipe his face every twenty or so seconds as the stuff felt sticky, uncomfortable. He could see a little better now and got up to a respectable forty on the soaked flats.

He couldn't have been off the highway more than twenty minutes when he heard a sound. Very dim at first—like a far-off airplane propeller—then louder as he cruised on. It was more than one thing creating the noise, not airplanes but cars, he realized. It was rare to hear a whole bunch at a time, as cars were an oddity in the new America. Most motor vehicles were no longer functioning, and those that were didn't have gasoline to run them. Gas was nonexistent. Stone had only the bunker's supply and one other hidden hundred gallon tank that his father had set up. After all that was used up he'd be in the same boat as the rest of the sinking world. Yet here someone apparently obtained enough octane to get a whole little fleet of them going.

Stone suddenly heard shooting and debated whether to go on straight ahead or check out the sounds that were coming from the low hills to the west a mile or two. His decision was to keep going—he had his own problems—

and he did, even giving it extra gas to get out of there. But as the firing continued he could hear it sounded like one gun was returning the fire of a dozen. Now that wasn't right whichever way you looked at it. Against his better judgement, Stone whipped the bars to the right and pulled back on the accelerator so that the bike shot forward as though it wanted in on the action too.

It took only a minute to get to the top of a row of hills a few hundred feet high, and he came to a stop as he reached the peak and looked down over the far side. It was a vast canvas of beauty and death. Stone could see for miles, the rolling hills far to the east, a lightning storm sending down flickers of yellow. But it was the battle unfolding right below him that caught his eye. A single rider was on a motorcycle as big as Stone's and was tearing ass almost parallel to the row of hills Stone gazed down from. The biker was being pursued by four vehicles, just about the most ramshackle things Stone had ever seen, hardly more than mini log cabins built atop rusting frames. One of the "cars" had no frame at all, just some branches lashed down onto the axles. On them, four men were sending out a storm of death—bullets, arrows, and even a slingshot that one of them used to fling steel balls as fast as the eye could see.

Stone could see the biker clearly thought he had it made to safety as the figure sat up a little straighter and looked around as if to give a Bronx cheer as he pulled slowly ahead of the pursuing masses. However, the biker couldn't see what Stone could: two more cars were coming in the opposite direction right over the next slope several hundred yards off. With down-sloping walls on both sides of the escape route, the biker was being led into a trap. Stone made another split-second decision: he hunched down into the seat and pushed off with both feet, turning the Harley to max.

The bike shot forward along the top of the hill. Stone didn't think he'd been spotted by any of the parties concerned—yet. He kept low, pulling back so he could keep an eye on the whole scene unraveling. He'd have to time it all perfectly or it was a wrap before he even began. He saw the biker reach the top of the slope and suddenly catch sight of the two other attack cars, these as sloppily made as the main force, just branches and pieces of jagged steel all roped together around the wheels and the chugging engines. Clouds of oily smoke were sent up as they drove the metal bodies forward like lumbering rogue elephants.

The biker unleashed a few blasts from some kind of rifle he had tied to the front of the cycle, and one of the riders hanging on the side of one of the cars took a direct hit and went flying off. But then the biker did too. Stone saw his right shoulder fly back and a splotch of red appear on the black jacket, which had writing on the back that Stone couldn't read. Somehow the biker stayed on. And in a way that sheer perseverance made Stone feel that he had done the right thing. No one should die who fought to live so hard. He saw there was no more time and swerved the bike to the right, suddenly shooting down the slope right toward the fifty yards of open space between biker and the cutoff cars. He gripped down on the machine gun's trigger when he was halfway there, not wanting to give the bastards another second to peg in shots on the biker, who looked like he couldn't take another hit.

Stone's 50-cals tore up the turf between the approaching attack cars and the biker and created some confusion for them, Stone could see. They slowed down slightly and looked around trying to find out who was letting loose with the firepower. Then one of them sighted Stone coming down the hillside like a demon possessed. The men in the two cars instantly stopped their pursuit of the biker and both vehicles turned toward Stone like two immense sailing ships creaking and shaking with the turns. The foul-looking specimens on the backs of both vehicles began opening up with their various crude weapons, screaming wildly and pointing as Stone's bike bore down on them.

Though they clearly felt that it was Stone who was making the mistake as they laughed and shouted that the biker was crazy, that changed quickly enough as Stone let loose with another burst from the 50-cal and this time he was in better target range. The slugs tore across the front of one of the cars, sending out a whirlwind of blood from inside that splattered through the broken windows. The car lurched wildly away from its companion vehicle and veered over toward the slope, where it overturned and went skidding along on its back, crushing the three riders into a stew of red dirt.

But the other car, whether out of bravery or stupidity— or both—kept coming at Stone, who pulled his glance away just long enough to check out the biker. The rider had stopped and was standing by his bike kicking at it. The machine wasn't moving. Great! The rest of the five-car attack force was approaching rapidly from the south, and the biker took out his rifle from atop the stalled cycle and lifted it toward the approaching cars. Stone ripped his gaze back on the single attack car ahead. It was about a hundred feet off and he could now see the face of the driver and a man by his side, aiming a shotgun through the glassless windshield. Both looked like they'd been eating coal.

The shotgun fired and Stone felt a whoosh of lead pass just over his shoulder. He pulled the 50-cal again and swept it straight down the center of the truck. Guts and faces and stuff exploded out the window space in a gush of red. Suddenly Stone was past the thing like two jousting knights bypassing one another. He wheeled around and saw that the car was still moving along but out of control. He shot forward and caught up with it, leaning to one side as he came alongside the vehicle, which had slowed to about ten and was putting along like a little golf cart.

Stone made a strange sound when he saw what his slugs had wrought inside the thing. They'd been cut to pieces. Neither man had a face anymore or much of anything else for that matter. But that was their problem. He pulled up to the car, setting one foot inside of it, and grabbed hold of the bloody collar of the ex-driver, pulling him out the door and over his bike so the corpse fell with a splat behind him.

Stone saw that the second man's foot was wedged in on the gas pedal, keeping the vehicle going. Good, maybe he had a little special delivery present for the rest of the gang. Keeping the bike maneuvered alongside the ancient hybrid vehicle, he turned the wheel, bringing the car around in a wide circle, then he straightened it back out again.

The biker had dropped to one knee and was firing at the fleet of cars bearing down on him, which were unleashing their own stream of fire. Stone aimed the car toward the center of the approaching attackers.

"Come on—go faster, you rusting son-of-a-bitch," Stone screamed at the thing, though the metal wreck didn't seem to hear him, just moved along at the same ten miles an hour, happy as a purring cat. Stone let loose with another volley with his free hand on the bike handlebar, not so much to hit anything as he was still too far, but to let the biker know it was time to get the hell out of there. There was no need to make Custer's Last Stand. The helmeted head swung up and around and seemed confused for a second. But then when he saw Stone firing at the cars, not at him, the biker jumped up and began tearing ass back toward Stone as fast as his legs could move.

The four cars spread out about fifty feet apart and came in on them in a half circle, clearly an attack strategy they had worked out before, one that doubtless plenty of men had fallen to. But Stone wasn't up for a shooting match. Not when he had a mobile bomb at his disposal. He kept the steering wheel aimed right at the dead center of the advancing wolf pack of dilapidated steel and wood, and suddenly the dead copilot of the truck fell over right in front of the seat, his shattered body lodging on the pedal. The vehicle suddenly lurched forward, giving Stone barely time enough to pull himself away and avoid the bike getting tangled up and going down. The car surged, and as he saw its graffiti-covered back tear off he let loose with a continued barrage from the 50-cal, aiming down below to try to hit something good.

The biker ran past the driverless car, staying out of the

way of Stone's fire. The car kept on like it had a will of its own. As the four cars focused all their weaponry on the thing for a moment, Stone reached the biker running forward.

"Get on," he screamed, but the biker didn't need any encouragement. Stone could hardly see a thing beneath the dark helmet but the face smiled. Just as the car reached the front ranks of the four cars trying to pass around it, one of Stone's shots must have hit something, for suddenly the special delivery let out with a loud crack from underneath and it burst into flames. The flames moved so fast and intensely that they spread out in a wall on both sides, extending out a good twenty feet. The nearest two attack vehicles were caught in the blast and their unprotected gas tanks ignited as well. Each went up in violent blasts of steel and smoking flesh.

"Hang on," Stone shouted, wheeling the bike around in a 180 so they could just get the hell out of there in case there were more of the slime.

"I'm hanging," a voice shouted back from inside the mask. And Stone knew instantly it was a woman. In spite of himself, even as he accelerated and tore away from the flaming scene, he turned his head for a second to look. Holding onto him with her left hand the right hand shot up and pulled the visor up on the helmeted head.

"That's right, I'm a woman—any problems?" a beautiful but tough-as-nails face sneered back from within.

"No, no problems at all," Stone said softly, and turned forward, not daring to say a word to his backseat passenger, like the most henpecked of husbands on a Sunday outing.

CHAPTER
Eight

"**S**TOP, I have to take a leak," the biker woman without a bike said suddenly after they'd gone about five miles and it was clear that the cars weren't about to follow. "Fighting always makes me have to pee," she added by way of explanation. Stone stopped and she jumped off. He could see the back of the black leather jacket she wore had the words "THE BALLBUSTERS" written in bright red on it. She walked twenty feet behind a scrub brush. Not that it gave much cover. She squatted down and let out with a contented sound, then walked back to the bike zipping up her tight jeans. She came up to the bike and gave Stone the once-over real slow up and down.

"Raspberry Thorn," she said, crossing her arms in front of her and tilting her head slightly. What with her jacket and studs on her wrists and long scar that ran across one cheek she looked just a little bit tough. Stone sighed.

"Martin Stone," he replied, taking his hands off the bars as he saw they were going to have a little conversation. Now that he thought of it, it seemed like a good idea.

"Why the hell did a tough guy like you go and do an asshole thing and save someone you don't even know?" she asked looking at him suspiciously.

"Oh sorry," Stone replied, "hop on—I'll take you back there or to wherever there are more of your 'friends.'"

"Slow down pardner," Raspberry replied, looking at him
through squinted eyes. "Just want to know why. You know
what kind of world we all live in."

"I helped you because my father—as stupid as it sounds
—taught me to live like a man," Stone replied a little angrily. "And that includes helping people when you can.
You know, all that kind of bullshit." He glared at her deep
blues. Stone wasn't used to seeing such natural beauty
under such a hard shell. If she smiled he'd be in trouble.
She smiled.

"Well thanks then," Raspberry said, her teeth glistening
like pearls. She suddenly seemed incredibly seductive. All
her features softening. And Stone did a double take wondering where this new woman came from. She even looked
different. "That was very brave—and since I'd rather be
alive than dead—I'm glad you showed up. Now if you'd
be so kind as to take me to my camp—then that would be
very, very civilized of you."

"How far?" Stone asked skeptically. He had wanted to
reach Amarillo tonight. The sooner he got to April, the
more possibility she'd still be alive. God knew what the
Dwarf and his sadistic crew were doing to her. They would
take out their anger at Stone on a girl who had never hurt
anyone in her life. But *they* know how to hurt. Stone had
already felt the sting of their sadism.

"Only about an hour to the west. Pleeeassse," she said,
tilting her head even more, pouting her lips. Stone could
see she'd trained in the art of man manipulation.

"Sorry, sister," he replied slowly as he would have liked
nothing more on this earth than to have taken her up on it
and spent the night tight around those luscious curves, his
face pressed into her falling mane of blond hair, which
spilled out from beneath the helmet. "I've got to go save
someone else—my sister. She's more important to me than
you are, to be brutally honest. But you can make it back
from here in a day. You seem to know your way around. If
you travel at night you—"

Suddenly she moved in a flash faster than Stone could

react to and was on the backseat behind him, a blade held around his throat pressed hard against his neck. The knife was sharp, razor sharp, and Stone could feel it digging in already.

"Move, Stone," she said without anger but firmly, and he knew she would use the blade if she had to. And she knew how to.

"Hey, slow down," Stone laughed falsely. "I was just about to say—but—I'd be glad to take you anyway." He reached slowly forward, gripping the bars as he thought for a moment about trying something. But the angle was bad, the blade was already digging in so that if he moved it at all it might slice real deep. He'd have to wait.

"Which way?" he asked, easing the bike slowly forward.

"That way," she said, pointing with her other hand so her fingers were right by his eyes. "Along the hills the way I was heading when the Jalopios took me down."

"Jalopios?" Stone asked. "You mean those slugs riding those fucked up trucks and cars back there?"

"Yeah, the Jalopios. They run this whole part of the territory for about fifty miles to the east. Until you get within twenty or thirty miles of Amarillo. Then the Tribunal takes over. Me and my gang had our run-ins with these Jalopios before. Usually they don't come this far west. They're dumb as shit but somehow they got themselves a whole damned fleet of junk. Though you managed to give 'em a nice hurting. Got to congratulate you on that again," she said, patting Stone on the shoulder. That's great, he thought—getting stroked on one side, knifed on the other. When they said women had two faces, they sure as hell knew what they were talking about.

"You mind if I ask you a few questions, nothing personal?" Stone asked as they drove through the mid-afternoon light of a gray day.

"Sure, you're cute, ask away," she said cheerfully enough, keeping the blade right up against his flesh so that when he went over bumps in the prairie the edge actually sawed back and forth and dug in even more. He could feel a thin trickle of blood already oozing down his neck and onto the top of his sweatshirt.

"Who are the Tribunal who rule Amarillo you mentioned?"

"The freaks. You never heard of them? Everyone in Texas fears those bastards. They're—ruthless. Make the toughest of the gangs out here in the badlands look like kids fucking around. The Greenshirts—the Tribunal's enforcement squads—come out sweeping up people. You never see them again. Just gone. Some say they're used for terrible experiments, that they cut them up and sew them together again. Others say they eat them. Who knows."

"Where are they located?" Stone asked, finding it hard to speak as his throat was a little constricted from being nearly cut into sandwich makings.

"Well, they don't want no one to know. But I know, 'cause me and my sisters we had our own run-ins with these Greenshirts before. So we spied 'em out. Found out they got this whole operation underground about ten miles south of Amarillo. An old missile complex or something. It's underground. Completely impregnable. Why, we dropped a few petrols down on top of the entrance grates, which were closed—and we couldn't even get a decent fire started. Then these automatic machine guns rose up right out of the ground and started firing at us. There wasn't even no one manning them, just spraying out a whole shit-load of slugs and turning back and forth real fast. We got the hell out of there. Always meant to go back and do some real damage."

"Well I see we're on the same side," Stone said with artificial cheerfulness.

"I never said we weren't on the same side," she laughed. "Of course we're on the same side." Stone didn't like the sound of the laugh. There was a mocking quality to it like she knew something he didn't—and it was pretty damned funny.

"You ever hear of a young woman named April? April Stone, eighteen years old, no—God—she's nineteen now," Stone said, realizing her birthday had been just weeks before. "Blond hair, blue eyes."

"Stone, you know how many missing girls there are in this state? More is missing than ain't missing. Why *I* was missing when I was younger. Kidnapped by half a dozen different groups of slimebags until I finally managed to kill the last ol' bastard who kept me tied up under his bed and came out here and joined the Ballbusters. We don't let no one mess with us or we—"

"Yeah, I get the picture," Stone said quickly, not wanting to get into graphic detail of just what they did to their enemies. He wondered even harder if he should try something but the woman seemed too good, too strong. He knew somehow she'd killed before and wouldn't hesitate, even though she seemed to get along with him in a way. Stone wouldn't have a chance. It took about two hours to get to her encampment and the sun was just setting as they arrived at the edge. Stone didn't see much at first other than about two dozen cycles parked in a circle, but as they drew closer up to several fires that others of the gang were standing around, he saw with amazement that they had dug their homes in the earth itself and topped the holes with windshields from cars, trucks, whatever. He could see the lights of candles and lanterns sending up jaggedly dancing illuminations from within some of them. They were spread out over the dark field past the two main fires, with car doors well-built right into the earth that could be swung open and closed. Talk about functional architecture, Stone thought, impressed with the cleverness of the operation. Just a hole in the ground—some automobile wreckage of which there was plenty around—and presto: instant all-weather home.

But if the earth homes were unique, Stone's eyes opened wide when he sighted the bizarre shape that stood between the twin bonfires. A mound of mud and earth stood nearly fifteen feet high. But more than a mound, a phallus, carved into the shape of a male organ at full extension. And two more mini-mounds below that stretched out for yards.

Around it women were venting their spleens, slashing at it with knives, spearing it with long staffs, shooting at the head of the thing, which, with its many holes and pock-marked craters, had obviously been attacked many times like this. What in God's name had he stumbled into here? Suddenly Stone's groin area tightened up like it was going into deep freeze. The whole kit and caboodle knew something was up. You couldn't hide a thing from Martin Stone's body parts, no siree. That was one of the things he really liked about himself. He was so sensitive.

The mix of hate and desire sent by the flashing eyes of the other women nearly sent Stone toppling off the bike as he brought it, under Raspberry's command, to a full stop about twenty feet from the main fire. Seated around the blaze on various car seats half fallen apart were the leaders of the band. Stone could see that immediately by the garishly painted antennae the leaders held in their hands like royal scepters, and the fact that all the other women were standing while the three of them reclined. The trappings of power were obvious in the strangest of places.

"Well look what Ms. Thorn done gone and snagged herself," one of the seated women spoke up with a nasty laugh. "A man."

"That's right a man," Raspberry snapped back as she stepped off the bike keeping the knife carefully around Stone's throat so he had to step slowly off too. "And he's mine. He saved my ass. The Jalopios were about to get my sweet tail but good, when this dude showed up on the scene and kicked butt. I mean he sent them into ketchup city, girls. So I want him."

"You know it ain't that easy sugarlips," one of them said, rising up and swaggering around waving her antenna. "We *all* gets to share. This here sisterhood is a de-moc-ra-cy. I say it would be more fun to roast the son-of-a-bitch. We ain't roasted no man for a long time now."

"Roast your clit, Rose Spike," Raspberry snarled as she kicked out a leg and tripped Stone down on the ground like one might trip a calf in a rodeo. So unexpected was the move that Stone went down, though he was able to stop himself before he hit hard with his arm and thigh. The camp filled with laughter and his face turned bright as a baboon's rear end, though none could see it in the waves of light and shadow from the fires.

"Don't you just wish you could," Rose Spike said, reaching down to the seat she left and grabbing a bottle which she broke against a rock. Holding the antenna in one hand and the ancient jagged-edged Ballantine bottle in the other, she came forward in a crouch.

"You stay down there, man," Raspberry commanded Stone, and she kicked him in the side to let him know who was boss. Stone pulled back a few feet and looked around but the number of them with pistols drawn and knives out just waiting for him to try something quickly dissuaded him from the idea. Raspberry reached inside her jacket and pulled out a pair of nunchakus and began whipping them around in a blur.

"You bin' asking for this for a long time," Raspberry said, circling around her adversary. "I bin' lettin you get away with a lot of shit 'cause you and me used to be tight. But lately—you a superbitch. So let's get it on, woman. Do your best."

"Sugarlips, you're about to lose your sweetness," Rose Spike laughed and slashed out suddenly with the antenna. The thing zapped out like a fencing épée so fast Stone could hardly see it, but Raspberry's nunchakus moved just as swiftly and slammed the antenna away. Rose Spike slashed out with the broken bottle from the other side and the swinging wooden sticks ripped into the bottle. It exploded in Rose Spike's hand, making it turn bright red as the glass dug in.

"Oh, hurt your widdle hand," Raspberry mocked the bigger but older and slower woman.

"Not as much as I'm going to poke holes in that pretty little body of yours, bitch," Rose screamed out. She flicked out with the antenna again and again, jumping all around. She was good—and a few of the slashes hit into Rasp-

berry, making her wince with pain though she didn't emit a
sound. Each spot the antenna struck a red welt appeared
and blood oozed out. But she was able to shield her face
until Rose Spike faltered for just a second and stepped back
to regain her balance.

It was Raspberry's turn. She came in swinging the nunchakus like a propeller blade and drove her adversary
straight back about ten feet. Then she flipped one end of a
stick up and the tip slammed right into Rose Spike's left
eye. It ripped the whole orb right from its socket and sent it
flying through the air in a spray of red that gushed out from
the hole. Rose let out a scream that everyone in camp
heard, heads rising out from beneath the car window
homes to see what the hell was up.

Rose Spike clamped both hands over her face, letting the
antenna fall, as if trying to stop the stream of red that was
pouring down her face, neck, and black leather clothes.
"My eye, my fucking eye," she screamed. Suddenly she
turned and ran right through them, stumbling over things,
screaming every inch of the way before she disappeared
into the shadows at the edge of the bonfire's light.

"I told her not to eye my men," Raspberry said to the
onlookers. "So she lost one of her eyes to even do it with.
Now she's a cyclops. Once more—she'll be a noclops."
She laughed loud at that one. And about half the others
joined in. And Martin Stone, lying on the ground, wondered just what he had had in mind when he had rescued
her. He should have tied her up and handed her over to the
Jalopios. They obviously knew how to deal with women
such as these.

CHAPTER
Nine

"**C**OME on man," Raspberry said, lifting Stone up by the hand until he was standing. Before he could move an inch she had slapped some cuffs around his wrists and pulled him off like a bound calf heading for the slaughter. Other Ballbusters went over to the great mud phallus and began shooting away at it to relieve frustration. She led him about a hundred feet into the shadows until she came to her own little bit of heaven dug into the earth. She reached down and pulled on the handle of the door entrance and lifted it up and back.

"Down man," she said, apparently in no mood for bullshit. Stone leaned over and found the top rung of a ladder that led down and climbed in. It was amazingly warm inside considering the chilly temperature outside as night fell. Raspberry followed right behind, closing the door of the place as she came down the ladder. She walked around him and lit a wax candle in the center of the dirt room, sending out a shifting curtain of yellow light. It was cozy down here, just the opposite of what Stone would have expected Raspberry to own. Frilly bedspreads and lacy curtains were draped all around the circular dugout home about twenty feet in diameter. It looked more like a New Orleans brothel than the dirt home of a biker queen.

"Like it?" she asked as she undid her jacket and threw it to one side.

"Lovely, lovely," Stone answered sarcastically, though he did admire the placing of two car windshields side by side to form a huge skylight overhead through which one could see the stars coming out as the high thin clouds melted away. "Place like this with a view and all must go for at least $100,000, ten percent down, right?"

"Built it for two dollars—that was to pay Big Tits for some of these satiny things she had found a box of. I like it to be soft and cuddly when I'm in-ti-mate." She looked deeply at Stone and he sighed as she ripped off her sweatshirt underneath the jacket and two melon-sized breasts swung out into view, stiff nipples pointing right in Stone's direction. He gulped hard.

"Listen Raspberry, my dog, he's on the back in one of the steel boxes. You didn't see him—he's covered up. But I'm worried about him. And if some of the others—not your friends of course—found out there was a male dog around—you know what I mean?"

"And you're right about that. Males of any species are never allowed in camp except for breeding or eating purposes. They'd make dog food out of him fast." She tore back up the ladder, opened the door at the top and yelled something out. One of her lackeys went running off into the darkness.

"It's okay now," she said, sliding down the ladder. "The bike will be put next to my other war bike. She will guard it. None will dare touch it."

"I thought your cycle got taken out there in the combat zone," Stone commented as she walked over to him with a come-hither look in her eyes, her bare breasts shining in the candlelight, wearing only the skimpiest of panties. These women were completely and certifiably schizophrenic, Stone was one hundred percent positive about that.

"That was my scouting bike. My war bike—that's here. No one gets near that. That's why I know they won't do nothin' to yours. You saw what I did to Ms. Spike tonight. They don't mess."

"I bet they don't," Stone said softly. He was thinking again about going for his guns, which were inside his jacket, difficult to reach the way she had him cuffed.

"Now don't you worry about that silly bike of yours," Raspberry said, coming up close to Stone until she was only inches from his face, her nipples touching his jacket. She took out both of his guns and placed them on a shelf, then turned back and up against him again. "Worry about pleasing *me*. 'Cause when I ain't pleased, you can see what happens, can't you?" Stone wasn't sure he liked where the conversation was going or not, though his hands had the strongest urge to reach up and grab a palmful of the perfect breasts that swung before him, daring to be touched, begging to be touched.

Suddenly she reached out and tripped him backwards. The woman was as fast and strong as many men he'd fought. Stone fell backwards, bracing himself for the hit. But when he landed it was onto the soft velvety spreads and pillows all around the place like some sort of Hugh Hefner bargain basement. He prepared himself to kick up as she attacked but she was down on top of him before he could make a countermove. And she wasn't exactly in an adversarial mood.

She was all over him like a living eel, squirming and rubbing against him, cooing in his ear and licking at his neck and face. She undid his pants and pulled them down and Stone was immersed in a state of mental, emotional, and hormonal flux. He didn't know whether he was going or coming.

"Oh you are a man, aren't you," she said when she had exposed him to the elements.

"Last time I looked," Stone replied. She didn't answer as her mouth was stuffed with something that made it hard to talk. Stone groaned and arched his back as she swallowed him down. He had such mixed feelings about the whole thing that had he been given the choice he might have just gotten up and walked out. But he wasn't being given any choices. And the male organ has a will of its own. Against his mental commands it began to grow under her lips and tongue and soon filled her, driving him to the brink of madness.

"I want you now," she moaned out. "Maybe you'll be able to satisfy me as none of the others have. Maybe tonight." She brought her body up to his hips and straddled his flesh pole. She guided it into her sex, not even waiting to go slow or any of that stuff. The staff disappeared all the way to the hilt and she slid down, her legs as wide apart as they would go atop his arching pelvis. Stone didn't know where the hell he was—he just knew the thrustings of two animals locked in pure passion. Her body was like heaven, or a close approximation thereof.

They went at it like writhing things for many minutes, and then she was going crazy riding atop him like a bronco. She made a wild cat-like sound and threw her head back, letting out with a long high-pitched wail. Stone reached his peak just a second later and pumped up hard into her, making her rise right up into the air. She quivered all over, her eyes closed, and made mewing sounds as he poured all that she had stirred up from his depths into her deepest burning parts. Just as Stone's eyes rolled back in his head he swore he saw faces peering down through the window ceiling above them. But then he was lost again in the grasp of her womanliness, her doe-like sounds as she gripped him tight.

When Stone awakened he knew it was very late. He had that dull throbbing headache and tired eyes that felt like they were glued together, which meant it couldn't be past three. He heard her voice whispering in his ear, making him come out of his languorous sleep.

"Up, you've got to get up now. They're coming to kill you, Stone. And I won't be able to stop them. Ordinarily I would kill you myself. As you might have guessed, we take out the men we drag in after their usefulness is over. But *you*—you satisfied me. I can't kill you and destroy any chance of ever having it again. You've got to leave now." She helped him put on his pants and then hesitating for a second she took out a key from a shelf and undid the cuffs. "I know you could kill me for all this," she said, handing him his guns. "But I'm taking a chance."

He gripped them looking at her hard, and then slipped them on. "Why should I hurt you—you satisfied me too," he grinned, leaning forward and kissing her. "You might have been a little less insistent—but I guess that's the way it is with modern girls." Suddenly there were faces above them again and still naked-as-a-jaybird Raspberry ripped a shotgun from the wall and fired straight up into the glass, sending it flying, and the faces that had been staring down flying for cover.

"Out this way, they won't look for a few seconds." She lifted a flap of material from the lower part of the rounded dirt wall and Stone saw there was a tunnel. "It goes about a hundred feel straight back. Circle around to the right once you get out. Your bike is there. Good luck Stone. If we ever meet again I want your body—and I don't mean dead."

"It's been interesting," Stone replied, getting down on his knees and starting into the tunnel. "I'll send a post-card." Then he heard voices and a commotion behind him and moved down the mud-caked tunnel as fast as his hands and knees would carry him. He came out on the run and went right around to the side using trickles of light from the fires to make his way. He could see them all running from around the camp to Raspberry's window on the world and there seemed to be fierce hand-to-hand fighting going on between all the "girls." Whatever power struggle had been brewing had clearly just gone over the edge.

He spotted the bikes parked together—his at the end next to what must have been Raspberry's war machine by the size of it, even larger than Stone's with all kinds of firepower poking out. The woman who had been sent to guard Stone's bike was taking her duty seriously and patrolling around the thing with a handgun dangling at her

side. Stone didn't want to hurt her. She had after all been
doing him a favor. He picked up a pebble and threw it a
few yards to the right. She came to investigate walking
around the bikes holding the pistol at waist level. The moment she walked past him Stone jumped out and grabbed
her around the neck. He put on a quick choke hold, apply-
ing it for only four seconds, ten could kill. But four would
put her out for a few minutes.

He rushed over to the Harley and saw that it was undis-
turbed. Anxiously, Stone threw open the cover of the box
he'd been keeping the dog in. It was still there, as frozen as
a still life painting. He reached down and felt it. It wasn't
cold. As long as it wasn't cold. He pushed the bike forward, using his feet as the uproar hundreds of feet away
was reaching Civil War proportions. At least Raspberry
was going into battle well-fucked. Stone couldn't hope for
any more himself.

CHAPTER

Ten

"WELCOME TO AMARILLO, A TOWN OF LAW AND ORDER. TROUBLEMAKERS SHOT," the sign read as Stone slowed the Harley at the outskirts of town. It was hardly what it had once been in its glory days, Stone could see as he stopped the bike at the outermost block of houses and looked around. The bombs that had landed nearby had clearly taken out a lot of the town as well. But they had rebuilt here. In fact, unlike just about every place Stone had been to thus far since he had left the safety of the bunker, they seemed to have actually gotten it a little bit together around here. The buildings, though crude, were in one piece, some even with doors and shutters if not glass over the windows. By modern American standards the town was a veritable *Lifestyles of the Rich and Famous*.

He headed down the main strip, dousing his light as he realized the dawn was bright enough to see by now. Already, Amarillo's citizens were up and about, rushing off in various directions. Though they didn't look all that happy about things, faces tight and grim, they did seem much more industrious than those Stone was used to encountering. People these days were so lethargic and ready to crawl into the grave that they were already halfway there. These were a better dressed bunch than the average mountain man. Not that they were wearing Pierre Cardins, but the simple work clothes and boots they had on seemed whole, even fairly new. Something was going on.

The only thing he didn't like about the place was the smell. It permeated everything. A thick chemical smell like there was a plastic factory nearby. Stone drove slowly down the main street as stores opened on every side of him. He pulled the bike up to what looked like a fairly well-stocked used hardware store, parked, and headed in. The storekeeper, a portly fellow with a thick top of hair like a dirty mop looked over at Stone with not the most welcoming expression.

"What you want mister? Ain't got time to fart around right now. The night shift boys will be coming in from the oil fields. This is my biggest part of the day. Now what you want—or be out of here." The man bustled around trying to look important as he fiddled with his junk, which lined various buckling shelves around his fifteen by fifteen foot store. Stone had seen backwoods stores that had only two things. This guy must have had a hundred—knives, hammers, axes, saws, machetes, even a few guns. A lot of the stuff looked in decent shape.

Stone knew that money talked a thousand times louder than the greatest orator. "How much for that knife there?" he asked, looking over at one on a shelf with twenty different blades. One of them was a very thin, nicely constructed switchblade. Stone had always wanted one. He pulled out a silver dollar from his inner pocket, having found that the shine of the coins seemed to open doors. It worked again. The storekeeper stopped in his tracks, his hands putting down some cast-iron pots he was moving, and he stared at the coin as if it was his salvation.

"Well, why didn't you say so," the fellow said with a big salesman's smile as he wiped his hands on his dirty jacket and held out one toward Stone. "Thought you were just another of the riffraff who float through town. Like to look—but not buy. Like to take—and not pay." He looked down at the silver piece as if pretending not to but trying to check if it was real silver. "Men around these parts been known to take down the underside of pans or even old car doors and hammer them into silver dollars. Not that most of them look much like the real thing." This one did.

"Now jes' what knife was you talking about?" the man asked, as he stepped back from Stone and smiled beatifically.

"This one here," Stone said, lifting it from the pile.

"Oh that one, that's one of the best in the place," the man said, rubbing his hands a little too nervously together. "At least—at least that dollar you're holding in your hand." He looked up at Stone to see what the reaction was to the outrageous request. For a silver dollar in most parts could buy a man a whole cow or a horse.

"Ridiculous," Stone smirked. "It's not worth a tenth of that." He looked around some more as the storeman coughed and mumbled something about value going up as things were used up, how there would be no more of anything soon. How everything was a collector's item. Everything was the last of its kind. Stone tuned the guy out with his ears. He knew the noble truths as well as this bastard. He looked around and spotted an odd pen with a leather thong attached around it.

"What's that?" he asked, lifting the thing.

"Oh careful, careful," the storekeep said, taking it gingerly out of his customer's hands, smiling all the time. There was something about the scent of money that made store types' lips pull back to their ears, and their teeth loom and glisten like piranha. "This is a firearm, believe it or not. A .22-caliber single shot gun. See, you just hold the base of the thing here, and twist the little lever on the bottom. Fires a shell straight ahead. A gimmick thing. Not a real weapon but—"

Stone reached out and held it in the same hand as the stiletto. His eyes were caught by some medical looking bottles on the end of one shelf. Stone walked over with the proprietor walking closely behind, his eyes growing bigger by the moment as he saw his bank account swelling like a radioactive sore. He lifted one of the bottles. "Tetracycline, Megadose," it read on the side.

"Stuff work?" Stone asked.

"Just came in," the storeman said. "Two days ago. Some old prospector brought them in from a box he found in some ruins. Can't promise you they're good," the man said. "Don't want you to take 'em and then start vomiting up your guts and come looking for me to snuff out. I run an honest shop here, just want you to know that."

"Well, I appreciate the warnings," Stone said, smiling warmly at the guy for the first time. "There aren't too many honest around, that's for damned sure. How much for the whole lot—knife, little gun here—hope you got some shells that fit—and the bottle. Just one will be enough."

"Well now, that's worth more than one of them there silver dollars, mister," the man said, trying to get a hint out of Stone what he had in mind.

"How about we don't waste time," Stone replied, reaching back into his jacket and extracting two more of the shining coins. "Let's just say three of these and call it even." He threw them down onto the shelf and they rolled around the other bottle.

"Yes, yes, that will be just fine," the keep said, reaching out and grabbing the things for fear they would try to get away. "And I do got four more slugs what fits that little gun. I'll throw them in for free," the keeper said, holding the silver in his hand and looking down at it with a most happy expression on his usually dour face.

"And one more thing," Stone said as he looked closely at the mini-gun. "I want a little information."

"As long as it ain't about what I do with my wife after the lights goes out," the man chuckled, "I'll do my best."

"What's that smell? It seems to get stronger by the minute," Stone asked, slipping his newly purchased things into various pockets. He put the single-shot pen gun around his neck with its leather thong.

"'Course it's stronger by the minute," the man said.

"That's the morning wind shifting this way. We're getting the stench from the oil fields and refineries. It's like this almost like clockwork everyday. The winds come in and they back all the smoke into town."

"What the hell do you mean—oil fields?" Stone asked, hardly able to believe that large-scale industrial oil drilling was going on. No one had that kind of technical expertise anymore.

"Where you from, mister?" the keep asked, turning walking across the room to a vault hidden behind a baseboard. He opened it and quickly stashed the dollars inside. "The oil fields is what powers this whole part of the country. What makes this town have money for people to buy stuff, what makes the smell. It's the oil, mister. The oil."

"I can't believe there are oil wells—it's just not possible anymore," Stone said skeptically.

"Oh, they ain't got the old kind of big rigs out there—you're sure as hell right about that mister," the keep said, closing the safe, turning the combination lock and rising up again. "It was all fucked up by the bombs. But the oil—it still comes out. Oh, you have to see it mister, have to see it. It's hard, dangerous work. That's why they pays 'em good money to work there. They need men with brains, not your regular assholes wandering around who don't know which end of 'em the shit comes out of. They don't live long out in the fields but they makes good money while they do. That's why there's even a town here. 'Cause of that stinking oil."

"Who's they?" Stone asked as he heard a rumbling outside and a bunch of vehicles coming down the street still several blocks off. "Who runs the whole damned thing?"

"The freaks pal, the freaks. Damn, you must have been living up on Mars for the last ten years or something. They control everything around here. Run the oil operations, control this town, ship out refined gasoline in every direction. They're into so much I couldn't even begin to tell you. Trucks coming in and out from all over the country to their operation." Everything the guy said just brought up more questions in Stone's addled brain.

"Who are these freaks? Where are they?" Stone asked, knowing he was starting to get close.

"Oh, I don't know what they all look like, seen only two of 'em myself. Wish I hadn't. They're just—freaks. Twisted faces, arms missing—whatever. Heard tales of how some of the others look that'd make your blood run cold. Anyway they runs the whole damn show. You cross them, you're as good as dead. I just stays invisible in my little shop here, pays my one-third tax to their strong-arm boys and keeps me mouth shut. Don't tell anyone you spent that money here, will you mister? They'd tax it if they learned."

"I don't talk about my money matters," Stone said dryly. "Where is all this oil anyway?"

"About ten miles south of town," the storeman answered. "The fields anyway. No one knows just where the freaks are located. They got all kinds of entrances hidden around the area east of the fields, maybe another ten or fifteen miles. All of them guarded by all kinds of damn electronic stuff. Take my word for it if you don't want to mess."

"I'll believe anything you told me at this point," Stone said with a quick grin as he heard the cars getting closer, huffing and knocking like they were on their last wheels. He headed toward the door. "I see you got your morning business coming in. So you say just head south?" Stone said as the storekeep kept grinning, glad to start out the day on such a prodigious intake.

"Go to the end of town, hit the main road, just keep on it. Can't miss it. There'll be trucks traveling down the thing all the time. I told you the operation never stops. They keep it going twenty-four hours a day."

"Thanks for the goods—and the information," Stone said. "And you don't tell anyone that *I* was here asking questions—and I forget the silver."

"You got it," the keep said, walking Stone to the door

and opening it wide for entry of any oil men. Stone eyed the six old cars being driven up the street, which sent up thick black funnels of sooty smoke behind them. Clearly the grade of petroleum being used was of a low order. The cars looked as beat-up as they came, but the men looked even worse. They were covered in oil, black coatings of what looked almost like tar, from head to foot. Not that they seemed to mind it all that much as they whooped it up and hung out the glassless windows of their cars. They barely paid Stone a glance, nor the store he stood in front of, but headed down another fifty yards or so to the bar. They piled out of the cars, not even bothering to close the doors, and headed on in.

"Damn bar," the storekeep muttered as Stone mounted his bike and started up. "These oilmen always just want to get soused, instead of buying the things they need—like what I got for 'em in here. Ah I don't give a shit. Today you made my fucking day, mister. Good luck. Don't mess with them freaks now, whatever your business be, or you won't be buying things this way again. That's a promise."

"Thanks for the tip," Stone said and started the big Harley down the main street. It took only a few minutes to get through the town as it was only about twenty blocks long. Still, that was a veritable metropolis in this day and age. He followed the road out of town, and just as the keep had said, there were trucks rumbling by every few minutes. It was a regular superhighway, with the huge oil trucks filled to the rim as black liquid oozed out of the not-quite-closed containers and pushed even the thick Mack tires of the trucks down a foot or so.

None of the truckers paid him any particular heed, although he did have to veer sharply to the far side of the road each time they came barreling along as they didn't seem to care too much whether or not they sent his puny bike flying off into the prairie dotted with H-bomb craters like immense sores from a plague. He was just about ten miles from town when he saw several bomb craters very close up ahead. They looked a little odd, as if large parts of

them had been dug away. As Stone came up to the top of a
ridge and looked out over the range ahead he did a double
take.

Oil fields stretched off for miles. Black swamps of bub-
bling oil oozed up everywhere. There were no oil rigs of
the kind that he had seen in the past, but just men wading
around in the stuff with rubber suits on, shoveling it into
barrels, which were being carted off to furnaces of some
kind off to one side of the vast field. It was a scene out of
hell, with the black figures struggling everywhere like an
army of ants, looking as if they were going to be sucked
under at any moment. Chimneys topped crude-looking refining plants that burned with long tongues of blue flame
shooting up hundreds of feet into the sky, releasing smoke
and noxious odors that covered the whole region.

Stone let his fingers edge toward the trigger of his gun
just in case there was trouble ahead. As he drew closer to
the great oil swamp he could see what had happened. Two
bombs had gone off close to where there had been a whole
slew of real wells. The blast had sent every bit of equipment flying off like so many leaves in the wind. But they
had also ripped open the huge underground reservoir. Now
it bubbled up everywhere, an ocean of thick crude oil, like
taffy. He watched the men sludging through the stuff like it
was quicksand, filling buckets, then dragging them to huge
vats which were set on wheels and moved atop tracks of
some sort. The tracks, built up on wooden stilts, weaved
through the oil field and men were pushing great loads of
muck down the tracks over to the burning refineries a mile
off.

It seemed a waste of manpower, Stone mused, as he
watched the operation. Why couldn't they just use industrial equipment? But as he saw one of the men fall off a
track headfirst right into the swamp of black sludge, he
saw why. Men were cheaper. The slime who ran the show
didn't have the slightest concern for human life. The man
sank under, without even having the chance to scream and
there was not the slightest attempt at rescue, as it took too

long to grope around the deep sections of oil to find anyone to make it financially feasible for the operators of the field to do so.

Another worker was quickly put behind the steel-wheeled vat and with three other men there they continued to push their load down the tracks toward the refinery. It took only seconds to replace the dead. Even as Stone drove on, he saw a man with a bucket about a hundred yards in from the road step forward and disappear into the depths. The oil fields had been so torn up by the bomb blasts that it was uneven, jagged in its bottom ground. The going could suddenly get much steeper, like stepping off the Continental Shelf, only you couldn't swim in this stuff no matter how many merit badges you had. Not through one black inch. And Stone realized that was part of the fun of being an oilman. And he saw why they were well-paid and why they ran to the bar the moment they hit town. You couldn't get a brain-damaged mule to venture out in those black death pits. Only men.

CHAPTER
Eleven

THE stench got even worse as he drove past the chimneys burning off impurities in a dozen extremely primitive refining factories. Stone had taken a trip through one once in a high school class trip and he remembered how complex it had been with pipes and tanks running off every damned place. This thing looked more like a bunch of country stills for making moonshine. But somehow they were producing something. He slowed to a crawl to watch the fiery process and could see that out of the bottoms of the round stacks stuff was being pumped into waiting trucks that ate up whatever was slugged into their innards. It was hard to believe that they could be running vehicles with this stuff. He wouldn't put it in the Harley. No way, José.

Even as he watched, Stone saw guards on the inside of the gate that fenced the entire oil field start walking over to see what he was up to. They clearly didn't like anybody eyeing their operation. Stone didn't feel like talking and just turned the throttle up. The bike shot ahead and he kept it going fast for the next mile or so. No one followed.

The storekeeper had said just keep going past the fields to find the locale of the freaks. Stone could see why he couldn't be more specific than that. The place was a wreck. It looked as if some vast military complex that went on for miles once existed here. Steel pipes and the remains of buildings, fences and all kinds of high tech gear now rusted and twisted like yesterday's toys filled the landscape. He had to slow the bike down and slowly make his way through the obstacle course of debris, which formed immense mounds. Whatever the hell had been here had been big, and important. The area, like the oil fields, had clearly had the shit bombed out of it.

He drove the bike up a high mound of rubble that rose forty feet with a shallow enough angle so that he could throttle the Harley right up the side. On top he brought it to a stop amidst the bricks and pieces of steel frame and looked around. The wreckage extended off on every side. What the hell had this place been? Air force base, missile complex? All this was the same kind of steel and concrete debris as if it had been homogenized by some great wrecking machine. Stone had seen the mushroom clouds of some of those "wrecking machines." They did their job well.

Seeing that he was getting nowhere fast he parked the bike, kicking down both wide kickstands so the bike was well balanced on the somewhat uneven wreckage beneath. He went around to the back and opened the dog's box. The pit bull was still snoozing away like Sleeping Beauty. What the hell was the dog waiting for—for him to dangle a frog under its nose? Stone knew he was pissed off just because he felt so helpless. But how long could the animal not even eat or crap or do anything?

He got out the bottle of tetracycline the storekeep had sold him and broke the seal. He sniffed hard at the contents, making sure they didn't have that rotten smell that so much of what he found and opened did. Most of the leftovers from five and a half years ago when manufacturing had basically ceased, had reached the limits of their storage life. Stone took out one of his Spam tins. His mother had loved the stuff, finding ten thousand ways to cook and disguise Spam back in the bunker. Stone had hated every one of them. Now he was eating the stuff half the time because he had no choice. He mashed some of the pink meat up in a metal cup and then added some water, making it a gravy. He broke open four of the antibiotic capsules and sprinkled their white powder through the gunk, mixing it around until everything was all the same color and the whole thing looked extremely unappetizing. He knew if the animal was awake it would have raised quite a stink about having to chew down this gunk. It wasn't going to get the chance this afternoon.

Stone turned the dog's head sideways to make sure it didn't choke and started doling the stuff out in a spoon, one little bit at a time so it didn't drown on lunch. After every few helpings he lifted its head and moved its body and neck around trying to make it swallow. After almost half an hour only about half made it in. But Stone was satisfied with even that much. And when he opened the dog's jaws and looked inside nearly gagging from the foul breath, he saw that what had gotten inside had made it down the gullet. Maybe he should take up a second career of veterinary medicine.

By the time he was done Stone saw that although it couldn't have been past one the sky was already darkening quickly to the north. Another storm, just what he needed. He packed everything up and closed the dog in, noticing that he'd let the mutt get pretty dirty. He had to clean it up and soon. It was becoming a scandal how filthy the creature was, the wildlife for miles around was talking. He vowed to not let another sun set without giving the pit bull a bath.

Stone mounted up and eased the bike forward, riding down the far slope as if he were on a sled going down at nearly a sixty degree angle. Then the bottom of the mound of rubble evened out and guided him over the more evenly strewn out wreckage. He moved along slowly through the remains of a lost civilization looking for he didn't even know what. He'd know when he found it. A lot of the fallen structures still retained their original shapes and were bizarre-looking to say the least. Huge round steel globes, black boxes twenty feet high that had antennae poking out of every inch of their surfaces. Everything looked like it had been aboard the Starship *Enterprise*. Whatever had been transpiring here had been of the highest technological order.

"Star Wars," Stone muttered into the dusty breeze. Maybe this was the control center they were building to maneuver all those satellites and lasers, and whatever they were throwing up there just before the war and the collapse. If so, the satellites must now be wandering around aimlessly up there looking for Mom. Probably start falling down to Earth over the next few years, if they hadn't already. He prayed they weren't nuclear, too. Or there could be a secondary series of atomic detonations far after the original fact. That would doubtless tip Earth's already severely poisoned environment that much further to the side of total extinction and annihilation. What a legacy coming back to haunt mankind.

The remains were fascinating, and he rolled along at hardly more than a turtle's pace inspecting the larger debris of once immense and interconnected equipment—computers, telecom units. Suddenly amidst a pile of girders that had been twisted around into pretzels Stone saw a four-drawer metal file that looked almost untouched. He stopped the bike and walked over, reaching under and grabbing hold of the thing. It was heavy, but he dragged it sideways from beneath the bottom beam and set it upright. He opened the top file, and to his surprise, it slid right out as if wanting to release its store of information.

Stone leafed through the folders within and whistled. "Top Secret." "Ultra Top Secret." "For Security AAA Clearance Only." This shit was as hot as it came. He took out a few and looked through them. He was right—Star Wars. The most secret of several Earth control bases that had been set up. Diagrams of particle beam alignments, computer codes for directing satellites to release missiles. It was incredible, like a how-to book to blow up the world. When he got to the last file his eyes opened ever wider. He'd hit it.

NAUASC. *North American Underground Assured Survival Complex.* There had been a whole subterranean headquarters built beneath all this so there would be a control if the surface arrangements were terminated. Well, they had been right about that. The pieces were slowly coming together. But the puzzle seemed to grow more complex. Stone's head was spinning. On the last two pages of the manual he found the listing of six entrance locations, clearly pinpointed to the square foot on the grid map that was attached.

For the first time in days Stone started allowing a little hope to bubble around in his guts. This could be just the thing he had been looking for, an ace in the hole to gain entry to the complex. They weren't expecting him, the element of surprise—if he went slowly—could help his terrible odds a little bit. For somehow, though he didn't know where, April was down there beneath his feet, beneath the rubble. And she was alive.

It was difficult to really follow the directions of the grid chart in the booklet, because all the landmarks they gave as reference points—buildings, concrete parking lots, whatever, were now gone, or rather mixed together in such a stew that a super computer couldn't have put them back together again. But Stone was able to figure out what had been a few structures, even though they now lay on their sides. It took nearly an hour of constantly readjusting his direction but at last he came upon a large metal plate in the midst of the rubble. Only there was no rubble on the plate itself: it looked completely seamless, attached to the dirt around it as if it were fused into it. Stone drove the bike up to the edge of the ten foot wide square of steel. It was blackened on the surface but the charred coating was only fractions of an inch deep. Still, it must have taken some of the heat from the original blasts that had gone off nearby.

Stone got off his bike and had walked a single step to take a look at the plate when he heard whirring sounds coming from every side. And even as he spun around, metal fixtures began rising up out of the earth all around him. There were six of them and as he focused on the metal objects attached to them, his eyes dilated. Machine guns, robot-controlled, and every one was turning and aiming at him.

"Attention, this is an unauthorized area. Repeat—you have entered a No Access Zone," a tinny voice said over a hidden speaker. "Get back onto the motorcycle. Do not reach for a weapon or try to escape, or we will fire all the guns at once. You will be dead in less than a second." Stone looked around but for the life of him couldn't see the speaker. He noted the guns turning slightly in the air, rising, moving, adjusting their sights constantly even as he shifted an inch or two one way or another. Even if he got off any shots, which was highly doubtful, the things weren't even human.

"Now, move your motorcycle slowly forward until you're in the center of the plate," the voice commanded. Stone followed the orders. You didn't have to say "Simon Says" when you had six auto-controlled machine guns aimed at a man's nose. Once in the middle of the steel plate, the speaker rumbled again.

"Place your hands on the back of your neck with fingers interlocked." Stone didn't hesitate. He didn't know how much it took to get these robot guns riled up and he sure as hell didn't want to do any experimenting. Suddenly the entire steel plate began descending into the earth as the machine guns leaned over on ball bearing joints and followed him down, just to make sure there were no last-minute tricks.

CHAPTER

Twelve

A S Stone descended into the earth he looked up to see a second steel plate slide over the opening and the light above shrink into a narrow band and then disappear. He wondered if he'd ever see daylight again. He was in a shaftway with countless doors, which he passed as the elevator dropped smoothly down. There was a dim amber lighting recessed into the shaftway, just enough to see by. The descent seemed to go on forever and Stone knew what it must be like to be a South African miner and just keep going down as if there was no bottom. If he was heading into the Survival Complex, they had built the damn thing deep. But then they had been planning to be able to take a direct nuclear hit so they had to be pretty subterranean—a thousand feet or more. The craters all over the area, the wreckage above, showed that someone had sure been trying to ice their tails.

Stone felt his ears click three times on the way down and his throat get a strangely dry sensation. He was just debating whether to come out firing at the bottom like Rambo when the mechanical voice spoke out again.

"Keep your hands up, mister. The stress modes show you're thinking of trying something. Don't!" Stone didn't know how the hell they were doing it, but clearly they were monitoring everything about him—even his blood pressure. He couldn't see a thing, not a camera, wires, anything either on the steel slab or the smooth-sided shaftway that looked like it had just been built. Titanium alloy, no doubt. Stone had seen some of the super-hard metal that his father had employed in his munitions company in various armaments configurations. And that had been before the war. Whoever he was up against was far, far ahead of anyone topside. Stone felt a chill ripple across the nape of his neck and then back again. For some reason he felt like a kid all of a sudden, and that he had bit off a little more than he could chew. Suddenly the unit dropped down into a large chamber and there were bright lights and armed guards who were waiting for him with their SMGs at chest level.

"Hey guys, shouldn't have gone to all this trouble," Stone commented as the platform clanked into some kind of locking mechanism beneath him, and a whoosh of air hissed out, letting the thing settle down until it was level with the concrete floor. Stone did a quick scan of the place. He'd seen pictures of such. Underground getaways that the government had spent hundreds of millions, probably billions on. The cavern he was in was a cylindrical shape about forty feet across and Stone could see even from within the inset elevator shaftway that the subterranean world extended off as far as the eye could see in six directions via wide connecting tunnels. Stone could see men marching back and forth through them like ants. Jesus Christ, the level of operation down here was staggering. What the hell were they all doing anyway?

"Stand up," a voice commanded brusquely, and Stone jerked his head to the right. There were five men all wearing ankle-to-neck olive green uniforms with all kinds of patches and insignias on their sleeves and chests. They were apparently very image-conscious down here. All wore plastic glasses, not really sunglasses, but high-tech looking things with narrow slits to let light in. They covered the fronts of their faces so everything from nose to eyebrows was covered.

Stone rose from the Harley and stepped off and as he got both feet on the ground, turned a tad toward the back of the bike to see if Excaliber was all right.

"Face front or we fire," the voice said, not even rising in tone as if it couldn't care less whether they did fire or not. All the fingers tightened on their triggers.

"Whoa, easy boys," Stone said turning quickly around and making sure that they saw his hands were up and away from his weapons. "I'm not going to try anything—I'm not crazy. I was just going to mention my dog, he's on the back in a box and—"

"Don't talk," the head of the six-man NAUASC team, which their shoulder patches identified them as, said, stepping around the bike and looking in. "We'll take care of everything. Now stand, keep hands up." The head of the unit reached down and frisked Stone, taking out his two guns, which Stone saw go with a sick feeling. Without his equalizers he didn't feel too equal.

"Do you have any other weapons? Tell me now or you will be severely punished later."

"No," Stone muttered, wondering what the punishment would be—no supper, no TV for a month. Somehow he figured it was probably a little worse.

"Come!" the man of few words said as three NAUASC guards fell in on each side of him. They marched him forward down the corridor and Stone eyed everything, trying to remember the route back to the elevator with precision as his life might depend on it. He mentally jotted down an odd-shaped black steel doorway that they passed that rose overhead like a Greek column. Then an incomprehensible wall of chromium tubes that kept revolving. He used his father's method of keeping track of things—landmarks in units of threes—easy to learn, and almost impossible to foul up once applied properly.

The deeper they walked down the tunnel the more mystified and nervous Stone became. It was the sheer scale of the place that was hard to come to grips with. Every corridor they passed stretched off to a distant blur and every one was filled with streaming dots of humanity. All of them were so purposeful, rushing around, carrying papers, boxes, pushing large computers, machines on forklifts. What in God's name were they all doing down here? Confusion more than anything will cause fear. Confusion and not knowing what the hell's going on. Stone found his backbone stiffening up with every yard of concrete walked. The dudes down here were awesomely powerful. He felt like an ant waiting to be squashed beneath a million-ton boot.

"This way," the head greensuit said, as the little column made a sharp left and headed down another cylindrical tunnel, this one slightly smaller in width than the main thoroughfare. The place was high-tech enough to make a yuppie, had there been such a thing anymore, have wet dreams. Recessed lighting in the ceilings sent down an even amber curtain over the tunnel. Seamless concrete walls reinforced with dull black steel beams were set right outside them every twenty yards or so. And what got to Stone even more than the Buck Rogers gear itself was the fact that it all worked, every goddamned bit of it. Not a light out, not a concrete section caving in. And this in a world where most towns didn't have lightbulbs anymore, let alone electricity, and where he hadn't seen a shack that wasn't caving in.

They walked on another hundred yards or so and then came to an immense steel door that was sealed shut. Two machine gun posts built right into the wall with only barrels protruding from concrete slits sat on each side of the steel doors. The head of the unit guarding Stone exchanged some words with whoever was inside one of the machine gun nests and then slid a plastic card through a steel slot in the wall. After another ten seconds or so, green lights blinked on and off in the walls on each side of them and then with a whirring sound that made the very cement beneath their feet shake, the immense doors slid open. They must have been five feet thick and solid as the inside of a mountain. They sure as hell were protecting whatever was on the other side.

Stone was marched through the doors, which began closing the moment the last man had passed through. The place they were entering was much larger than anything he'd seen thus far, a square room a good two hundred feet on a side and perhaps twenty feet high. There were ticking machines, maps lit up like neon lights, all kinds of communications equipment beeping and blinking like mad. Stone's eyes darted back and forth trying to make heads or tails of the whole operation. He felt like a monkey in a cyclotron.

Suddenly he saw ahead, the far end of the room was empty of equipment but for a long black steel bench about twelve feet above the floor at which ten men sat staring down, waiting for him. It was more subdued lighting at that end and Stone couldn't see all that clearly until he was within about fifty feet of them. Then he saw all too clearly. The freaks. The ones he'd been told about. He couldn't see their full bodies, just their heads and shoulders—those with shoulders—for all were seated in their places behind the bench so they were more or less poking up about the same height above the thing. They were hideously ugly, twisted like they'd been put through meat grinders more than once. And sitting in the middle, his armless egg shape clearly silhouetted by a greenish light thirty feet behind him on the steel wall—was the Dwarf.

"Thanks so much for coming," the Dwarf spoke in high-pitched timbre as he looked down from the steel heights.

"Kneel down before the Tribunal," the head greenshirt standing alongside Stone said, suddenly slamming at the back of his legs with a truncheon he pulled from a clasp on his side.

"Oh, he's an old friend," the Dwarf laughed, "no need for the usual formalities." The guard pulled back instantly, stopping a second blow in mid-swing. The rest of the guards stepped a few feet away from Stone, but made it clear that if he tried anything he was fertilizer. Stone took a quick 180 of the place looking for any exits. He saw nothing, just the same seamless metal walls and on various high emplacements resting on metal platforms, gunners, cameras, machine guns ready to deal out a fusillade if the need arose. These guys were better protected than the President had been.

"God, do I wish I'd done you in when I had the chance," Stone said without malice. To him the little monster was a disease, it was beyond a personal thing.

"Ah, but you didn't and therein lies the very fickle path of history. For I am alive—and you—well, for the long run, I must confess your chances don't look too good."

"What are you guys, casting directors?" Stone asked, sweeping his eyes back and forth over the uglies, "looking to get a crew together for your next monster picture, no doubt."

"Yes," the Dwarf squeaked, "we are monsters. In body and soul. What is the darkest thing there is?" he asked, looking down at Stone through black pinpricks of eyes.

"You Dwarf, no doubt about that," Stone answered, keeping his arms clasped behind his neck as he saw every guard watching him close.

"No, Stone, the darkest thing of all is when a man loses the last thing he has, the last thing connecting him to this earth. And for you Stone, that's your sister. I'm going to marry her Stone. The lucky woman has been chosen to bear my children. To be my—queen."

In spite of himself Stone lost it completely and rushed straight toward the high bench. So many guns were trained on Stone that the "safety off" clicks could be heard echoing off the steel walls. At the very instant they were about to tighten the triggers a voice screamed out.

"No! The man who fires will die hard." The fingers relaxed quickly. They all knew what the Dwarf had done to those who failed or annoyed him. "He can't reach us," the egg-shaped man went on. And it was true. Though Stone made it to the base of the steel bench, knocking down two of the greenshirts who tried to grab him, he couldn't begin to reach the freaks. Within seconds, even as he clawed madly at the hard surface, the guards overpowered him, knocking him to the ground. When he rose thirty seconds later he had bruises around his face and his hands were tied with nylon behind his back.

"There, feel better?" the Dwarf asked with mock concern. "Get it all out, your little tantrum. Don't worry, Mr. Stone, you're not going to die, at least not right away. I have all kinds of plans for you, oh yes I do. Not the least of which is that you're to be my man of honor at the wedding ceremony. I've been counting on it." The Dwarf laughed again, sounding like a teapot whistle going off. The sound made Stone cringe. He felt sure he was going to lose it all. He wondered what it would be like to just—crack.

"What the hell's going on down here, Dwarf? Who are the others? What—"

"My, you are an inquisitive fellow, aren't you?" Dwarf replied, pointing his right stump at Stone. "But all in good time, my man of honor. We have many, many things to discuss. We shall dine—tonight or tomorrow perhaps. I'll have to check my schedule. I didn't know for sure just when you would be arriving, you understand. But meanwhile let me have our men make you comfortable, let you freshen up a little. Take him."

The guards grabbed Stone under each arm and began dragging him away from the Tribunal chamber. He struggled furiously, his mind a boiling red rage of fire and fury. He wanted to kill the bastard, with his bare hands if he could. But what drove him to the point of total despair was the fact that April was so near, maybe just behind the wall. And he had no way in hell of reaching her.

CHAPTER
Thirteen

IT could have been Frankenstein's laboratory. Stone didn't like the looks of the place the moment the guards dragged him roughly inside. The place had clearly been designed as a medical facility from the start, nothing makeshift about this. The walls were all stainless steel, glistening and mint. There were beeping life support systems, tubes and wires, operating tables, rows of scalpels and cutting implements, like a surgeon's warehouse. The place had been built for the rich and powerful of America who had hoped to survive down here. They hadn't, but their medical facility taking up an entire twenty thousand square foot level of the place had.

"Face forward, scum," one of the guards screamed, slamming the butt of his weapon into the side of Stone's head. Only because he was able to pull his head with the blow did Stone avoid a serious injury, but it hurt like a bitch and his eyes clouded up for a few seconds as if he'd been sniffing onions. When they cleared again he knew he was in trouble.

As they passed into a second operating room with five operating tables set up around the rounded, brilliantly lit chamber Stone saw that bodies were lying on each of them. And they had been cut up terribly, sliced into parts and then reattached with thick thread. He could see immense stitches around shoulders, elbows, knees, even a neck. War victims? Transplants? He could barely try to imagine what it all meant. But it was hideous, as if someone was cutting up human bodies like they were paper dolls to be twisted and mutilated.

All of them were in terrible agony, moaning and tossing their heads this way and that as if undergoing the most exquisite tortures imaginable. Clearly whatever was occurring here had been going on for a while. Some of the stitches looked many months old. And as he walked on, his eyes clearing a little more, Stone saw that it was worse than he had first realized. The limbs were all twisted around—elbows on backwards, knees pointed to the inside. Stone saw that one of the poor bastards had had breasts implanted onto him, another an extra arm that had been sewn to his abdomen. The groans of these had an extra element of suffering in them.

Stone thought he was going to puke. But even as he felt the bile rising he told his stomach that his head was going to get hit again for sure if he upchucked all over the nice green suits. And his head wouldn't like that at all. His stomach subsided.

"Here, scum," the guard behind him said as they entered another room. This one was as large as the operating chamber, but it contained electrical equipment, all kinds of implements that looked as if they could be used for torture. "Welcome to your little personal entertainment center," the greenshirt laughed. Stone was led to a long stainless steel table that had no one on it. They pushed him into a sitting position and then slammed him back down on it, reaching out and tying his hands and ankles at each corner of the thing. They then stood back, letting their weapons lower now that he was immobilized.

"Ah, you're here, my timing is excellent," a voice suddenly spoke out from behind the guards, who quickly stepped out of the way and snapped to attention. They were clearly scared of the man by the sheer speed of their movements. But then, who wouldn't be scared shit of a bastard who ran an operation like this.

"Usually I'm late for things, I don't know why, I try to be on time. But it's a fact that all great men have always been a little absent-minded about details." Stone squinted as he tried to see the speaker against the bright lights, which filled the ceiling. Pain was so much better when lit up. Whatever Stone had been expecting to look into view was not what ended up standing before him. He didn't even loom, being only about five feet and an inch or so tall. He looked more than anything like an accountant, bland-faced, tightly combed hair, suit just so, brown and boring, everything so innocuous it was as if he might just sort of slip away and vanish against the apparatus around him. Hardly menacing.

"Allow me to introduce myself. I do believe a doctor and his patient should know one another, don't you?" He smiled a tight quick smile that made his eyes twitch a few times. Stone didn't return the gesture.

"I'm Dr. Wolfgang Kerhausen, head of surgical—and other procedures here in NAUASC. You and I will doubtless get to know each other quite well."

"Tell me, where did you learn how to inflict so much pain, bastard?" Stone asked, his face filling with flushed anger. "What you've done to those men out there is—"

"Is science Mr. Stone, science. I am a man who is trying to advance the course of medical knowledge, of man's ability to transplant, to even grow new limbs."

"But the suffering you're putting those men through— it's not justified. Nothing can justify that."

"Ah, but you're wrong there," Kerhausen went on, as he motioned for his guards to get something and three of them rushed off toward the far side of the room. "All is justified in the name of progress. I learned that well at an early age from the greatest of teachers—the Fuhrer, Adolf Hitler. He understood that the use of war prisoners and Jews for medical experimentation was progressive—even humanitarian. I was a young doctor then with the medical corps. I was lucky enough to be drafted into Dr. Rulger's Jew Dissection Unit, where we were given all the living bodies we could handle for years. It was in the early days of microsurgery and transplantation—and damn, we learned a lot. Oh, I won't admit we didn't have our fun as well. There is much fun in pain."

"Not for me," Stone said, pulling slightly at his bonds to see if there was the slightest chance of escape. There wasn't. He was held down with steel wire that looked like it could contain a raging bull.

"Ah, but you like the others have no choice. That is the way it all works. The great universal system of master and slave. Some were meant to rule, others to be ruled and give their lives for and to the state. Some were meant to experiment, others to be experimented on. It is all part of God's plan."

"I don't think God has anything to do with your 'experiment,'" Stone said bitterly. "And I think when you die, you might be in for a big surprise."

"Yes, I probably will, won't I? I *am* looking forward to that. Quite curious. Anyway, we must get on with it. First of all, Mr. Stone, just so you understand what's going on. You're not going to die. Not right now anyway. The Dwarf has his own plans for you. But I am allowed to play with you for my own amusement, an appetizer before the main course. And knowing that you *won't* die, *can't* die, because the pain being produced is being controlled so precisely that it can bring you to within a fraction of an inch of going over the abyss, but it doesn't—oh, you'll see quite soon."

Guards wheeled a huge contraption with dials and hookups and cords with suckers on the ends of them. It looked crazy.

"I'm so proud of this machine," Kerhausen said, as his white-gowned operatives cut Stone's clothing free with scalpels and then attached the appropriate suction pads and clips onto him. "It's really quite amazing," Kerhausen went on as he walked slowly around the operating table looking down at Stone's naked body like a banker counting money in his vault.

"This is a new generation in pain production equipment. It's something I've been working on myself for the last four years, since the Council of Ten installed me as the head of Medical and Information Collection facilities. It's an all-purpose torture machine. That is, it will affect every part of your body, Stone, not just the skin or flesh, but every part—you'll see."

Stone wriggled around as they hooked him to the thing but it was a futile struggle. They had him tied down like a calf at a rodeo. They put a helmet over his skull which covered over his whole head down to the neck. Inside were earphones on each side of the thing and a kind of screen built into the helmet just inches in front of his face which he could barely see by the dim blue light it gave off. Electrodes were attached to various parts of his anatomy, including his testicles. Stone had to admit he felt fear, down to the very core of his guts.

"Can you hear me, Mr. Stone?" Kerhausen's voice came through the speakers inside the helmet, booming out. Stone didn't answer. "Hold onto your synapses." Stone dimly heard the click of a switch and then he was thrust straight into hell. Everything was exploding in on him. Sounds were booming and screaming like sirens and bombs all going off at once. Brilliant multi-colored lights were being flashed onto the screen directly in front of his face, causing his eyes to instantly feel as if they were on fire and burning horribly. But as bad as all that was, the pain shooting through his every nerve from the electricity being delivered to him at two dozen points was absolutely overwhelming. Especially his testicles. He could feel his whole body jerking violently around as his muscles pumped like mad, but because he could only move a few inches he kept slamming against the chains, which ripped at his wrists and ankles and throat.

There was no time with such pain. Just radiating torture pouring through everything in a flood. Stone tried to keep his eyes closed to at least protect them but the light was so intense that it went right through his eyelids like the rays of an atomic bomb. The sounds seemed to grow, getting higher pitched, screeching out with feedback and the shrillest of sounds. He thought his eardrums would surely tear under the wear. The agony was so intense, as Kerhausen had promised, it was hard to even know where to feel the pain first. It was as if his mind darted from spot to spot searching for escape but finding none.

Suddenly the device was stopped and his body collapsed back down onto the cold steel table, every pore sweating out sheets. He lay there quivering while his mind echoed back and forth in some other dimension, slowly coming back into this world. The helmet was lifted from his head and Stone was relieved to find that at least that was all for the moment. As his eyes painfully readjusted to the room light and he was somewhat amazed to discover that he could still see, Stone's heart sank down against his backbone. Now the bastard was standing next to a wheel-bottomed cart with Excaliber lying on it strapped down. The doctor was smiling that same razor-thin smile. The bastard truly did delight in giving pain—to men, animals—the slime probably choked daisies at night in his bed.

"And what did you think of our little multimedia light show, Mr. Stone? Did it live up to your expectations?" Kerhausen seemed genuinely interested in the answer as he clearly loved his pet torture machine.

"Don't hurt the fucking dog," Stone managed to croak out through cracked bleeding lips that didn't want to move.

"Oh, how sweet. He shows more concern for the animal than for his own flesh. A classic altruistic personality type. Just the kind the Fuhrer was trying to exterminate. Come, little poochie," Kerhausen said, scratching the unconscious animal under the chin as he pushed the cart it lay on. "Let's go to my animal lab for your own individualized treatment." As he walked off the white-robed lackeys reached over and placed the helmet back on Stone's head. Oh Jesus, no, he prayed silently, feeling his heart speed up in fear. The helmet was clamped shut and Stone lay there shivering against the cold steel beneath his back and thighs and naked buttocks, wondering just what the hell he had done in a past life to deserve all this. Then the click came again. And the pain with it.

Fourteen

STONE saw what the "doctor" had meant about it being a better thing to know—or at least believe—that you would soon die, for he surely wanted to die as the electric jolts seared ceaselessly through him. And the knowledge that he wouldn't, that they had it all gauged so well that they could take a man to the edge of death and hold him there for hours, was in many ways the worst part of the torture. Marquis de Sade with high-tech toys.

But at last the current ceased and his body dropped back to the operating table rippling with fire. The helmet was again removed from his head and Stone's ears and eyes felt like they had been put through a car wash of acid. He blinked hard, looking around, wondering what the hell they had in store for him next. A man was standing at the foot of the table staring at him. A freak with a dark grin across his ugly mug. The guy reminded Stone of the Dwarf in a way, same bald head, but this one had legs—and arms, though the hands on the ends of each arm, which ended about where the elbow was on most people, were two claw-like appendages that opened and closed as Stone watched.

"Feeling better, are we?" the little freak asked as he rubbed his claws together like a stockbroker at an all-widows party. "First the torture—then we eat," the man laughed. "I am Hans, the Dwarf's personal manservant. He has sent me to invite you to be his guest at his pre-wedding feast tonight. You're to be the guest of honor." The man freak motioned for the greenshirt to undo Stone's attachments to the table. "We've got some new clothes for you, as your others were so dirty." Stone was pulled up. He could hardly stand, his legs were like rotted matchsticks wobbling around in all directions. But again, they seemed to know what they were doing. The pain hadn't actually damaged him—after a minute or two he found, almost against his will, that he could walk and move.

Stone was allowed to put on the freshly cleaned and pressed greenshirt uniform and then his hands were cuffed again and he was quickly hustled out of the place under armed guard with Hans in the lead down the hall ahead of them. He led Stone to the elevator bank, into one and down a few levels. When the doors bingbonged open Stone swore he was back in Imperial decadent Rome.

Freaks, male and female, were everywhere, many unclothed or nearly so, running around drinking, eating, chasing one another. This was an anarchy of debauchery and excess in a world that was starving to death. Stone was led across the floor and he saw that some of the couples were actually banging away at each other right on the floor. He was taken to an immense round table covered with food and bottles of liquor and wine. Around it were seated the Ten freaks of the Tribunal, supported by pillows all around them while nubile and scantily clad young women, these not freaks, tended to their every need.

"Stone, you're here," the Dwarf said from his place at the table. He was squashed down between a number of huge pillows with two nude women who couldn't have been older than sixteen on each side of him holding food ready to pop it into his mouth. "The festivities have already begun, but they're not real for me until you've arrived. After all, you're the man of honor. But we'll save that little surprise for later. Please be seated." Stone was slammed down into a metal seat with low legs so he was almost sitting at floor level just a yard or so from the Dwarf. His hands were kept free, but his body was strapped into the bolted chair at three places, making him able to reach out to the table but not escape. The greenshirts stood back and waited their arms folded a few yards behind him.

"There, isn't that comfy?" the Dwarf laughed. Sitting so close to the little egg-shaped creature, Stone could see that the scum was even more repulsive than he had quite realized. Perhaps it was the jaundiced color of his skin, or the face itself, which was all swollen like something that had been waterlogged and then dried out again. The Dwarf poked his stump into the face of the teen on his right and she slid a wet, red slimy-looking thing into his mouth. He let it roll around inside a few times and swallowed hard with a look of sheer ecstasy crossing his face. "Goddamn, they're good. You've got to try one."

When Stone let his eyes fall to the bowls filled with pink and yellow and green things in front of him, he felt like puking. They were slugs and larvae, worms and beetles. The thing the Dwarf was eating looked like it was red and round and dripping with a sticky coating. The whole table was covered with such fare and the other freaks were grabbing it up in their hands and claws.

"I don't think I'm all that hungry," Stone said, looking full into the black rat eyes of the little murderer. "Your electroshock therapy didn't do wonders for my appetite."

"Oh you still don't understand, Stone," the Dwarf laughed as he leaned forward toward a small box set onto the edge of the table. "I'm not *asking* you to try some— I'm *telling* you to." He lunged out at the button with the tip of his swollen stump and Stone felt another surge of current shoot into him. He had the damn chair wired—that's why it was metal—to conduct the electricity. Stone jerked around within the confines of the thing. The jolt lasted only about four seconds but it was plenty. Stone had had enough of the hot juice back in the Surgery Department.

"Maybe I'll try one of these," he said after letting his brain and mouth fall back into place. He reached forward and took hold of one of the red slime balls and lifted it as slowly as a condemned man's feet down the final execution hall.

"Ah, wonderful," the Dwarf commented, pulling back from the controls on the hotbox and clapping his stumps together with fleshy sounds. "They're really quite tasty. I planned everything so carefully. I do want you to be pleased."

"I'm touched," Stone said as he put the "delicacy" against his lips. He closed his eyes and swallowed hard, trying not to taste it. It was wet and musky and extremely unpleasant, and Stone could feel its mucousy tendrils all the way down his throat.

"They're iguana testicles. They're terrible plain—but marinated in garlic and chives for at least a week—well, I tell you." The Dwarf squealed like a punctured pig. Oh, he was clearly in fine fettle tonight. They all were, Stone could hear from the constant backdrop of laughter, moans and wet slurping sounds. He made a quick perusal of the table as the Dwarf tapped at one of his female companions and she slipped another one of the veined grapelike appetizers into the eggman's narrow jaws. They were all here, all ten of the freaks. Nature's gift to mankind. Right.

He hadn't been able to see them all that clearly in the darker Tribunal chamber but here close-up with the harsh lighting everywhere, he could see it all. Every burn boil, every scale, every misshappen jello mold of a face. He could see the extra arms on one, the thick red tumor growing like a horn from another head. Every one of them was a nightmare. Stone wondered how they could look in the mirror. Maybe there were no mirrors around here. But the one that got to him the most for some reason in the midst of the feast of horror was the man whose face was falling. It was as if all his features were just dripping down, unable to hold their correct position anymore. The nose was down at lip level, while the lips had fallen almost to his chin. Both eyes had migrated a good three inches, and had drifted closer together so they almost appeared to be one big eye. The head had lost all its hair but had instead a thick spider web of dark purple veins that stood out and throbbed violently like worms. Yet he too was laughing, fondling the normal human girl next to him. They knew how to have their fun. Stone had to give them that.

"Now do try one of those," the Dwarf pointed toward a bowl of crawling white maggots that were half floating in ginger sauce with a parsley topping.

"I really don't think—" Stone began, turning his head away in disgust. He had a thing about maggots. He didn't even like to be near them—let alone eat one.

"Electricity is man's best friend—don't you agree?"

Stone reached forward before the Dwarf could poke his stump at the button. Stone just couldn't handle any more of that tonight. If he did puke, it would be their fault, though considering the kind of fare on the table, he doubted anyone would notice. He looked down into the bowl of squirming maggots. They wriggled around, swimming through the sauce as if looking for maggot heaven. Stone saw one of the little fuckers who looked stunned, motionless, and reached for the thing only to have it go wild on him the instant he lifted it up. He squeezed the white maggot hard and managed to get the head off of it before he brought it to his lips, which the Dwarf didn't notice. Stone slid the thing in and swallowed it whole, trying to pretend it was a clam on the half shell. Only clams didn't wriggle as they slid down your throat, trying to find a way to crawl out.

Fifteen

BUT if Stone had thought larvae and sauteed centipedes were bad, when the Dwarf slapped his stumps together a minute later and servants began carrying in the *big* stuff, he saw that he had only just begun to eat. Loaded onto an entire spit with six men holding up each end was an entire cow. It wasn't the biggest cow in the world, somewhat stunted in fact, but what it lacked in mass it more than made up for in physical accoutrements. This cow had two heads and six legs and it was nicely seared on the outside. The servants dragged the whole steaming carcass to the table and suddenly lost control of it, sending it careening down the middle of the round dining table, which then sent bowls flying in all directions. The freaks let out with uproarious laughter. They were apparently in their element with whole cows flying. They dug in at the steaming beef, the extra legs and head being the most sought after parts. Those that couldn't move had their girls hack them pieces with long carving knives and hand-feed it to them.

Stone figured cow, even a mutated one, couldn't be that bad, so he avoided a shock by leaning forward and grabbing a slab of meat that had flown off the thing in the manic cutting. He lifted it in one hand, seeing that this was not exactly the fork and knife crowd, and took a chew. The meat tasted strange, almost hot. And Stone knew it was radioactive. These bastards didn't care, they were all already mutated beyond recognition. They had nothing to lose. But Stone didn't feel like going out with a radioactive stomach, holes burned right through his abdomen with digestive fluids leaking out onto the floor.

He tried to pretend to eat the piece, each time making sure that no one was noticing. And beyond the Dwarf not one of them was paying any attention to Stone. He let his pieces fall to the floor just beneath the table. With all the meat and juices flying around there was no way in hell anyone would tell. They had barely gotten going on the cow when another crew came through the door hauling in something that looked like a fish, only it was huge, a good eight feet long, weighing at least two hundred pounds. And it was white, completely albino with no eyes. Stone had seen pictures of things like this caught from the bottom of the ocean, ugly deep-sea dwellers that were blind all their days. And good thing, for even this dumb overtoothed water thing would have had heart palpitations had it been able to see the crowd that salivated over it.

They heaved the fish right down onto the table and it flopped around a few times, landing alongside the cow, so that some of its protruding teeth sank into the lower charred hindquarters.

"Good shot, good shot," one of the freaks yelled out. They ripped chunks of the fish with their bare fingers. Stone could see that aside from being psychotic mutations they were all drunk and drugged out of their minds, eyes rolling around in their misshapen heads like balls in a roulette wheel. Suddenly the Dwarf rose up on his lower stumps, hopping around on his thick satin cushions as he held a cup of blood red wine between his stumps.

"And now for our evening entertainment," he squealed, spilling the cup as he lost control. "I present my theatrical piece: 'Death of the Ten Thousand Bites.' With the word "bite," one of his servants pressed a button and a pulley system hidden in the ceiling was suddenly activated. A box attached to a cable was about thirty feet up at ceiling level. The pulleys quickly lowered it down so that within a few seconds it was hovering right over one upraised leg of the cow just a few inches above it. The motor stopped and the draped box just hung there slowly revolving around. A greenshirt jumped up on the table, making sure not to get anywhere near hands of the slurping freaks and pulled the canvas cover from the box.

Stone gasped. A man was inside a plastic square about the size of a telephone booth. He was naked and looked terrified as he beat with his fists at every side of the box trying to find a way out. But even as all eyes rose from their debauched carrying on around the table it got a lot worse for the poor bastard inside. A second section of the booth, just above his head, suddenly opened up and gallons of insects, what looked like ants from where Stone was sitting, poured out all over the man's body. Within seconds they nearly coated him and the man was screaming his lungs out, going mad inside the plastic cage. Though he banged and slammed on the sides of the thing the Plexiglas must have been at least three inches thick, for it didn't budge an inch. His screams as well were completely absorbed within the thick material. It was strange to see a man moving his mouth with such vigor, his lips so wide it looked like they would crack—and not hear a bit of sound coming out. The ants were huge, red ants as big as a man's finger. They tore into the imprisoned man with a violent hunger. Within seconds hundreds of little trickles of blood erupted all over the man's flesh and a pool of the liquid began collecting at his feet. It was clearly going to take a long time for this particular "theatrical" event to be completed. Stone turned his head away in disgust and fury at the way these bastards used human beings as toys to be shattered and ripped apart for sheer sadistic pleasure.

"What is the sound of a scream that no one hears?" the Dwarf asked, turning to Stone.

"Disgusting, Dwarf," Stone whispered through gritted teeth, "it's just all completely disgusting."

"Wrong, Stone. The sound is your own heart beating in your chest. For you can hear that scream, can't you Stone? We can all hear it. The silent scream. It's the name of the Game."

Stone sat back in his metal seat, deciding that he would refuse to eat another bite of the diseased feast before him. He wouldn't join in their sick games any further. "Why do you get so much pleasure from inflicting pain?"

"Because we are diseased, Stone. Look at us. We are freaks. And we have been turned into this by a world that destroys all that it touches. The rule of humanity has always been that the strongest live and the weaker die. How ironic, that we the physically weaker, yet mentally stronger, shall live and shall become the dominant species. And just as our outer surfaces are twisted, the inner ones as well are labyrinths of pain that are beyond a mere mortal's understanding. We return to the world what we received from it."

"It's not the whole fucking world I'm talking about," Stone said, his voice rising in spite of himself. He addressed the suffering the man inside the Plexiglas booth was undergoing as he was being eaten literally one scrap of flesh at a time. His entire body was a blanket of ants now, only they were red and brown as blood covered their clawing mandibles. The victim scratched at the sides of the booth, his hands leaving red trails that were like a child's fingerpainting as they smeared around inside the transparent surface. "It's that poor bastard in there who you're doing it to right now. It's the electric shock you gave to me. It's God knows what you're doing to my damned dog and my sister." Stone glared hard at the Dwarf, his face burning with rage.

"That's entirely right," the Dwarf replied, his own face shriveling up like a raisin too long in the sun. "We shall rule with pain because pain is what humanity understands. You've been out there, Stone. They're a bunch of worms, ready to be pushed over by the first two-bit warlord who comes along. We shall unite the land again under our rule.

There will be order. All shall be quite peaceful, I assure you. Oh, some will have to die for various reasons, but most will live. And we shall ensure a restructuring of America—a better one. Then the Game shall be won. And we shall see just who has won and who's been left behind." He poked his stump at one of his handmaidens for another squirming bit of foulness from the table, which he gobbled down so lustily that little moving legs fell from the corner of his mouth down to the satin and velveted fabrics that lay beneath him.

"What game is that, Dwarf?" Stone asked, lying far back in his seat. Even the scent of the "meal" was sickening to him now. Forget where Jimmy Hoffa had disappeared. He was here on this table in the meatballs, Stone had no doubts about that.

"The Game we play down here in our little world. The Game of Go. You've heard of it, no doubt, a Japanese board game. But we've added our own variations. We have immense electronic boards that show each of us just where and what our holdings are around America. All is entered on computer. What each man's power, his holdings, armies, assassins—whatever—is worth. We have worked out an elaborate set of equations for the whole thing. It is all beyond your ability to fully fathom, I assure you. There are many levels of the Game—from operations in the badlands—drugs, slaves, whores—to our own internal game that we play on a hundred foot board here, using sets of rules that make chess look like bingo. This is because we play, Martin Stone, with the very world."

Stone was silent. He knew somehow the man wasn't bullshitting. He meant those words. The very world.

This crew, with the weaponry and troops at their disposal, really did stand a chance of taking it all over. If not all, then tremendous amounts anyway. Who was going to oppose them? He hadn't seen a single force out there that even came close to matching just what he'd seen since he'd been below ground.

"And you, Stone, are part of our game. Oh yes, you

certainly are, you—and—" He looked up, stopping for a second, staring into the Plexiglas cage. The man inside, though he was undoubtedly still alive as the ants couldn't have penetrated to his inner organs this fast, had fallen to the bottom of the cage and was no longer moving. Stone could see even from where he sat tied up that the ants were already starting to work on the eyes and were crawling into the ears. They must have preferred those parts, for they were battling violently over them, slashing at each other. The Dwarf squealed again with delight.

"I did so want to time everything perfectly. And now the best part of the evening, the reason in fact why we are gathered together to celebrate," he cackled, and now he was going full speed, his face a mass of twitches, his stumps waving wildly in front of him like they were searching for the missing ends. "To celebrate my engagement and my betrothal. To—your sister, Stone. And isn't she a beautiful bride-to-be." The Dwarf waved his arms at a greenshirt who was standing behind them and a second Plexiglas square was lowered from the ceiling. The thing came down and stopped about a yard to the right of the now completely ant-covered man whose outer layer of flesh was missing so that the muscle and gristle and everything that's usually hidden underneath could be seen oozing as the ants dug ever deeper with gusto.

The cover was ripped from the second box and Stone's eyes widened in complete madness. April was inside wearing an obscene bridal gown made of white satin. Only her breasts were poking through holes that had been cut into it, and other parts were exposed as well. It was like a porno queen's idea of a wedding dress. She was in a trance, her eyes open but staring unfocused and straight ahead, her breathing slow and deliberate. They had drugged her out of her fucking mind. She hung there spinning slowly before him and Stone felt his mind starting to go.

"She's such a beautiful bride, isn't she?" the Dwarf said almost tenderly.

"To the Dwarf," the face fallen man across the table

suddenly yelled out as they all looked on for a moment out of their drugged revelries. "May this bitch bring him many worthy man children. And may every one of them be as ugly as he is." He raised his glass high and the others joined.

"Come Stone, drink, for you are to have a place of honor at the ceremony." The Dwarf raised his stumps and poured the drink down, half of it spilling down his chin and chest.

"You bastard, you fucking slime-coated bastard," Stone screamed. And then he was screaming nonstop at the egg man and all his pals and writhing around in the metal chair like a madman in a straitjacket. And they were all laughing and pointing at the Dwarf who raised his glass high as if to signal victory. And Stone somehow knew that in this insane Game of theirs, the more he screamed the more fucking brownie points the little bastard got.

CHAPTER

Sixteen

STONE screamed all the way back to his cell and then screamed some more. He cracked. Between the food, the ants, his sister and every other goddamned thing, he just let the walls go and it all came out in insane curses and threats, none of which could be carried out. Then he tucked himself into a corner of the square steel cell they had thrown him in and at last fell asleep, his body shaking even in dreams from the aftereffects of the electric treatment. When he awoke at God knew what hour of the night, he tried to lift his snoring head from his chest where he had passed out. He felt like shit, with drool coming out of his mouth and a terrible smell in the room. He remembered last night and suddenly a flood of rage went tearing through his chest. But even as his heart speeded up from the charge of adrenaline he heard a sound, a bark in the grayness of the room and turned with a sudden surging hope in his heart.

It was Excaliber. The dog had been nosing around the far corner of the twenty foot square they were in. The animal came flying down the steel floor when it saw that Stone was awake but slightly misjudged its trajectory as it came hydroplaning in and slid right past him, slamming into the metal wall about five feet behind Stone. Same old mutt, fearless but not quite getting his angles right. It was incredible—the bastards had actually fixed him up. The dog seemed good as new.

"Good dog, I thought you were finito, for Christ's sake. What the hell have you been up to? Your wound, let me see it." Stone got down on one tired knee and pushed the animal's fur aside around the chest area. The wound looked much better now, the stitching had been replaced with tight catgut stitches. Already it looked like the dog's hide was growing together in places. Excaliber barked hard and licked Stone with a great swipe across the face and then another fast. Stone smiled for the first time in days. With the dog by his side, somehow, he inexplicably felt like he had a chance in all this.

"Amazing, isn't it," a voice said from behind him and Stone turned around. Dr. Kerhausen's face was peering through a small opening in the door. "What a few stitches here and there will do. His aorta had been cut slightly you know. Whoever did the original stitching did a good job, but not quite good enough. There was blockage in the passageway that was allowing only about a tenth of normal blood supply to get through. So the canine went into an unconscious hibernation. A typical reaction, actually, for many creatures that aren't getting enough blood flow."

"Well, I thank you for helping my dog," Stone said, holding onto the animal's neck like he didn't want to let go of it again. "But you're still a fucking butcher."

"Oh please, such an old-fashioned word. I am a scientist. All that I do is for and in the name of science. All. And in that regard I'm going to need a few samples of you and your dog's tissue and blood," the doctor said, pressing a button in the outer wall. "But I'm sure both of you would put up a most ferocious fight if I tried to bring you out— we'll just use a little of this NX7 gas here—and presto." There was a hissing sound and Stone got the whiff of something sour and very chemical smelling. And almost the instant he smelled it he was falling into blackness.

When he awoke, his head was splitting. This time he was strapped down to a medical chair, his head and arms, everything firmly locked in place. He could see Excaliber as well out of the corner of one eye, and another figure under a sheet on the other side of him, this one stretched out on an operating table.

"Ah, I see you're awake," Kerhausen said with a grim, tight smile. "Not to worry. I'm not going to be cutting you up or anything like that—today. Just taking some samples so I'll be prepared when I do get to you. I'm sure the Dwarf will let me have what's left of you after the Games —and the dog too. I have such an ambitious idea for you both. I'm quite excited about it." He reached down and took a scalpel and cut into Stone's arm before he could even move it, not that he could jerk the thing more than a half inch in any direction.

"There, just a little blood and tissue sample," he said, taking the surgical blade and slicing out a little half inch patch of skin right off the arm. Stone gritted his teeth hard, but he wasn't going to give this bastard the satisfaction of showing him any pain. He knew they got their kicks out of it, all of them.

"There, not so bad, was it?" He patted Stone on the shoulder and then walked over and did the same to Excaliber, who put up much more of a response than Stone had and wriggled furiously, twisting his head wildly at the air as his jaws were muzzled.

"There we go, all done," Kerhausen said cheerfully as he took both samples and put them in frozen storage, into a bin from which steam rose. "Liquid nitrogen," he said from across the room. "Will keep it perfectly preserved until I get a chance to cross-culture it and do all the other boring things that go into every surgical experiment. In fact you might be wondering just what I have in mind, Mr. Stone. I'll show you." He ripped the sheet back on the figure to the side of Stone. There were two figures, a man and a woman, both of them conscious, apparently, as their eyes were open—both were totally immobilized. Some kind of muscle relaxant must have been pumped into them because they weren't moving an inch. Both were all primed up for operations, with lines drawn over their bodies in bright red ink.

"You see before you the man/woman transplant. I'm going to put all the woman's parts into the man. Create a new being, something that has never existed before. And then, Stone, it will be you—and your dog's turn. For I shall implant parts of him onto you. My boldest project yet. The first animal/human transplant. They're freaks here, Mr. Stone. And they want only other freaks around them. And soon, soon you shall be the biggest freak of all. Half man and half dog. Oh, I can't guarantee that you'll live very long. But while you do, it will be a most historic and interesting occasion, I'm sure."

Keeping Stone all tied up with no place to go, so that he had to watch every revolting bit of it, Kerhausen had his whole operating team assemble around the two figures next to him lying on the wide table. They were both hooked up to all sorts of support systems, breathing, life monitoring, anesthetic tubes. And then the operation. It wasn't pretty. Whole breasts sliced right off like they were the sides of a turkey at Thanksgiving dinner. And then sewn onto the chest of the man. Then all of the women's other sexual characteristics were transferred. Breasts, hips, and even her sexual organs were cut out and sewn into a space made in the man alongside his own sexual apparatus. Everything was squeezed in tight. It was insane. It was impossible. But it was happening right before Martin Stone's wincing eyes. The first man-made hermaphrodite. And what a bloody mess it was.

Seventeen

WHEN Stone awoke he came punching and kicking right out of his dreams, where he was smiting the bastards left and right. But when his eyes opened with a start to his own frantic flailings, Stone saw that he was back in his metal-walled cell and wasn't smiting anyone. He heard a sound from a corner of the room and was startled for a moment until he remembered that Excaliber was back among the living. And looking his usual early morning hungry as shit and pissed off as hell.

"Dog," Stone said in a whisper, as the mere sight of the animal made him feel a strange kind of secret joy. He had been so sure the pit bull wasn't going to make it that now he had to admit that he really did care for the little fucker. As wild as the dog was, he was more loyal, and intelligent as well, than most of the homo sapiens Stone had been bumping into. Pitiful comment on the human race—but true nonetheless.

"Come here you little shitkicker." Stone grinned and the animal came bounding across the floor with unbridled energy. It hit Stone square on the shoulder as it jumped up with a little too much enthusiasm. Stone went flying over backwards with the dog's stinking paws all over his face and chest.

"Jesus, animal!" Stone shouted, pushing the dog off of

him and rolling to the side. "You make feeling sentimental a combat action." The dog came charging forward again, tongue hanging out like it was scraping the concrete floor for insects. Stone stood up fast. Excaliber wasn't a dog you could pet sitting down. Suddenly there was a sound from one of the seamless walls and a door slid open. Two greenshirt guards walked in and stood side by side with nasty looking pump 12-gauge Brownings trained on Stone and the dog. Excaliber started to growl, as he never had liked the sight of anything metal pointed at his face.

"Easy dog, just take it fucking easy," Stone motioned the animal, and it slinked off back to its corner again where it sat down and kept two pissed-off looking eyes pasted on the guards.

"Stand back," one of the greenshirts said, motioning Stone to move. "Feeding time." Suddenly right between them a small misshapen woman walked in carrying a large box on a strap over one shoulder. It was clearly heavy and she stumbled into the room nearly tripping. Stone started forward to help her but the guards lowered their death-dealers with sudden movement. Stone just looked at them with disgust and helped the dwarf woman take the box from her shoulder and put it down. She looked Stone right in the eyes with a puzzled expression. She was old and very ugly, like her face had been cut up for a dissection class and rearranged several times; her body too. Yet somehow within her pain-filled eyes Stone saw thanks. He smiled at her.

"Food," she said, kneeling down and opening the metal box. "For you and the dog." At the word "food" and the sudden scents wafting out of the box Excaliber was up in a flash and toward the chow case. Stone had to grab him to keep him from knocking over the woman. When it came to food, nothing dared stand in the way of the animal and its culinary destination, be they cripples, old women, or both.

"Slow down, dog," Stone shouted, grabbing it by the ears and pulling it backwards. "All things comes to those who wait."

"Thank you," the woman said, looking up at Stone with some surprise. Apparently she wasn't used to too many folks extending even the slightest courtesy to her. Stone could see that when the guards, yelled out for the old hag to hurry up, as they had other mouths to feed. She opened the box and took out two large steaming bowls filled with stew and placed them down. Then a gallon jug of water, and some fruit.

"The Dwarf said to feed them well," she said, looking around at the guards who seemed to be a little bit suspicious of such good eats as the other prisoners didn't get nearly so much. She winked at Stone, pushing the things forward. "Meals are twice a day. Does your dog have any special requirements?" she asked. She looked around again at the guards, this time sneering at them, so her teeth showed, and Stone saw that there was quite a nasty creature dwelling inside that wretched body who would strike back when pushed to the limit. "Dwarf said to feed the dog too," she spat at them. "They have to be strong for the Games." The two guards grumbled.

"Well just hurry up, ugly dwarf bitch," one said. "We haven't got all day." She handed Stone the water jug and then closed the box and put the strap back over her right shoulder. Stone helped her get the weight up; once she was moving forward it didn't seem too bad. Again she gave him a look of silent thanks and then she and the guards were gone, and the door slid noiselessly closed so Stone was sealed in again as if into his own coffin.

The pit bull was slobbering up a storm around the bowl like there was no tomorrow. Splattered food reached as far across as the far wall and Stone had to retreat to one corner and sit on the floor. The food was good. Really good. The best chow he'd had since the Sunday nights in the bunker. That was when his mother used to cook them all kinds of good things from the frozen vaults that his father had filled with thousands of pounds of frozen meats and vegetables. Five years they had been in there and they hadn't used it all up. But Stone had to admit, eating fresh food was far preferable. The stored food had been getting a kind of stale taste in it, like it was turning to dust, which it all was.

Absolutely nothing happened for the next two days, other than the dwarf woman's reappearance with food twice a day. Other than that Stone tried to keep active by running around the cell, doing jumping jacks, pushups, stretching, shadow boxing. The dog ran with him, and though there wasn't a hell of a lot of room, the two were able to get in a decent amount of exercise. Stone knew he had to keep at the peak of his reflexes, or as close to it as he could muster. Whatever these bastards had in store for him with their Games—he wanted to be ready—for. He wasn't too optimistic about either his chances or April's. But the thought of the Dwarf marrying her—and her bearing his children—was so hideous and repulsive an idea to Stone, that every time he even thought of it, it made his whole stomach feel like he had just swallowed a gallon of sour milk. And he thought of it a lot.

Mid-afternoon of his third day enclosed in the steel cage, the door opened unexpectedly between feedings. Stone, who had been standing on his head in a yoga position for upper neck and shoulder relaxation, was so startled that he fell over onto his side, which got Excaliber all stirred up and growling so that the whole place was in its usual chaotic state.

"Shhhh!" the dwarf woman said as she hobbled through the door and aimed a small transmitter at it from the inside so it closed quickly behind her.

"I want to help you," she said as she came to the center of the cell, limping on one foot. Stone saw that she was virtually crippled in every part of her body. It was as if every single joint had been bent out of its proper angle and alignment, every tendon twisted. Stone knew who did work like that. She stopped just before him and smiled as Excaliber relaxed, seeing it was the Chow Lady. He came up to her and rubbed his nose into her hip in a gesture of supreme friendliness. The animal rarely did that to anyone but Stone.

"He likes you," Stone said with a grin.

"There isn't much time," she said, her voice trembling with pain as Stone realized that all those terrible woundings of her body didn't just look peculiar, they hurt like hell. "The Dwarf—you know he is planning to have you compete in the Games. They start tomorrow. You have less than twenty-four hours before—" She hardly seemed able to continue.

"What?" Stone asked "What are the Games like?"

"I have seen other men compete," she said with sobs catching in her throat, as she had obviously seen many people come and go down here. "But none came out alive. The Dwarf sets humans against beasts they have no chance of defeating. Against lions, and immense alligators. He has units of troops out constantly scouring the territory for hundreds of miles just trying to get monstrous creatures who will rip and tear men in different ways. I don't know just what he has planned for you. But it will be terrible, I can promise you that."

"What—what happened to you?" Stone asked, hesitant to delve into such a personal subject. Yet he couldn't help it, for her mutilations looked inflicted by men, not nature.

"I . . . I . . ." she stuttered, hardly able to talk.

"Easy," Stone said, "you're among friends." The dog snorted and pressed his nose deeper against her hipbone as she scratched the furred head.

"They took me—and—destroyed me," she said, tears starting to form at the edges of her eyes. "Dr. Kerhausen used me as one of his first experimental subjects when he arrived here. I was a secretary once for the Under Secretary of the Air Force. When the war came, we were all placed down here. There were hundreds of us—at first. But something went wrong. Many died, became mutated, burned. There were gases and radioactivity. I don't know. The ten are all that are left of the original bunch. And they are freaks like me. Freaks. They stamp the image of themselves on all that they touch. They wish to make the world diseased and ugly. Dr. Kerhausen ripped me apart, sawed my very bones from my body and then reshaped them. In the name of science, he said, over and over again, as I screamed and begged for mercy. Science has no mercy, he would answer over and over again. It cannot. The individual must be sacrificed so that society can survive."

"Jesus," Stone said, looking down at her with horrified eyes. He knew that as bad as he might ever feel, what with his mother and father dying and all, there were others, like her, who had undergone far, far worse.

"I don't know how I survived. Most don't and they are discarded, or ground up and used for nutrient solution in the hydroponic sector. Nothing goes to waste down here," she said bitterly. "But I did live and Kerhausen let me live, because he wanted to see what would happen to me as the years went on—what would happen to the twisted bones, the rewired nerves. And gradually they let me wait on them and trusted me enough to serve them food and clean their toilets. And I have waited, Mr. Stone. Waited until I knew I could hurt them, could get them back in some way. And that moment has come. I want—to help you, however I can. I want to kill them all. What they've done to your sister—it's horrible. Drugged her, and the blasphemous wedding dress—degrading every sacred institution of the old world. They had me cleaning in her room—I saw her."

"You know where she is?" Stone asked excitedly, suddenly realizing that the dwarf woman could be his ticket out of here. She could change the odds from impossible to just a million to one.

"I know where everything is," she said, letting her lips curl back over her teeth, which Stone saw were filed down by the mad doctor for some reason. They were sharp and looked like they could hurt when she finally cracked and leaped at one of their necks like a wild rabid beast. "I've become just a thing to them. A Quasimodo who carries buckets and food, who fetches shoes and cleans and mops the halls. You don't know how long I have waited for this day," she said with a most determined expression on her wizened, burnt little face.

"What's your name?" Stone asked softly.

"My name?" She looked confused. "I haven't used it for so long—they never call me by my name." She had to think for a few seconds and then a smile crossed her face, a strong real smile for the first time since Stone had seen her. "Elizabeth," she said. "Elizabeth Hopkins."

"And a nice name it is," Stone said, holding out his hand. "I don't think we were ever formally introduced. Martin Stone, and—"

"And Excaliber," she said quickly. "I know all about you two. As I said I can go everywhere—even into the Dwarf's private information files. I'm like a flea beneath contempt or notice. I've read the dossiers on many people who have passed through here. Yours was one of the largest. He hates you, Stone. Hates you more than anything in this world. He truly believes that when you're dead there will be nothing left that can stand in his way to total domination. And with you gone, and the Tribunal's control of the space missile systems, they'll—"

"Whoa, hold it right there," Stone said, holding his hands up. "The missile systems—what do you mean by that?"

"I thought you knew." She laughed. "I guess there's no reason to think that. In my mind, as I read about you over the last few months I guess you became my—" she blushed and looked up shyly like a young girl. "Heroes know all."

"Oh Christ," Stone groaned. "Please, no hero stuff. I'm too fucked up myself. Too many vices, neuroses and cowardices lurking in these bones."

"Anyway," she went on, looking nervously at the door and then back again. "Aside from this complex being a survival operation, it was also the control center of the entire Star Wars missile defense system. That includes over a hundred atomic missiles that can be targeted on any part of the Earth. From controls down here in this station they can launch anywhere, anytime. They are going after nothing less than world control. Like Hitler all over again. The

Ten Hitlers. And with the missiles, as I'm sure you can imagine, they'll be able to take out anyone who gets in their way. There will be thousands, hundreds of thousands like them—and me. A world of freaks and burning ruins. That is their vision. And that is why I will help you—to destroy them. I only pray that I get to drive the stake into the Dwarf bastard's heart. I ask only that you give me that pleasure if God help us we ever get that far."

"You've got it," Stone said, hardly able to speak, feeling the sheer waterfall of hatred inside the twisted woman.

"Now tell me what do you need? Quickly, I've got to get out of here. If they catch me with you I'm dead on the spot."

"All right," Stone said, dropping to one knee and placing his hand gently on her shoulder. She wasn't used to being touched, just hit. And the contact made her pull back for a moment.

"I'm a monster and shouldn't be touched," she said, turning her face away in shame.

"I've seen worse," Stone said. "Now, I need a map of this place—of particularly April's room, the missile command, the Dwarf's quarters—and a way out. Preferably alternate routes to all of these places as well. Any weapons storage you've seen. And if you can get me a pistol, anything like that. But the map is most important. If I know where I'm going—at least I won't be traveling blind."

"I'll do what I can," she said, slipping away from him and aiming the transmitter at the door, which whooshed open. She looked both ways quickly up and down the hall and then was gone. The door started to close behind him. Stone had the sheerest instant of wanting to leap through the opening and get out of this claustrophobic place. But he wasn't ready—he had to have the map. He stared back at the now sealed wall and just sat and waited. And he wondered if the fate of America itself rested on the twisted shoulders of an old dwarf woman.

CHAPTER

Eighteen

WHEN Elizabeth came the next morning with food, but with the guards present behind her, she winked at Stone as she handed him his usual bowls and water for him and the pit bull.

"The Dwarf said to give you an extra serving today," she said. "With all the trimmings." She handed over the extra plastic container and then stood up. "You'll be missing dinner tonight, for you have a three o'clock appointment with—"

"Shut up, dwarf bitch," one of the greenshirts shouted, kicking out at her with his boot. The blow sent the dwarf woman flying sideways with a strange sound coming from her throat. Before any of them could move an inch Excaliber launched himself into the air and fastened his teeth around the offending boot, dragging the guard down onto the floor where the bull terrier proceeded to shake the living shit out of the dwarf kicker.

"Don't shoot, don't shoot," the man on the floor screamed out at his companion, who was trying to get a bead with his 9mm. "The Dwarf will kill us both if either of them are harmed."

"Get off him, Excaliber," Stone shouted, reaching down and pulling the dog up by its tail and one back leg and dragging it backwards. It released the boot with some reluctance. The greenshirt was trembling and staring at them both with hate-filled eyes. It was clear he wanted nothing more on this Earth than to be able to blast them into non-existence at that very moment. But he couldn't.

"Let's go," he screamed at Elizabeth, who had already gotten up from the concrete floor and was heading toward the door. She smiled quickly at Stone as if to let him know that she was okay; indeed, she had suffered a lot worse than that. This time neither guard laid a hand on her. Stone waited until the door had shut and then waited another thirty seconds just to make sure that there wasn't going to be some sort of sudden peek-a-boo. He gave the dog its chow, not wanting a stampede, then opened the extra bowl.

His eyes glistened with hope. A long icepick, industrial strength, solid as a rock, and a good twelve inches long. Nasty and lethal as a hand weapon could get. And next to it, crudely drawn on a piece of white linen used for the Tribunal tablecloth, she had drawn a map of the different levels and the locations of the places Stone had requested, plus a few more. Like where the boiler system was, the Dwarf's secret emergency exit, little things like that. She'd come through like a pro. It felt good to heft the icepick and stab out at the air a few times, testing the weight and balance of the wood-handled weapon. He could hide it in his sleeve, and then whip it out in a flash. Possibly not even be noticed handling the weapon if he moved quickly. Next to a machine gun it was the perfect choice.

Stone had a few hours before the blessed event, and he found himself growing increasingly edgy. The dog too somehow knew something was very nearly up. Not that it minded a good fight, just that it didn't like the unknown. And it could sense Stone's discomfort and anxiety as he paced around fast trying to figure it all out. But there was nothing to figure out. Stone had to go into battle—and most likely he was going to die. And take the dog down with him. He tried to calm down, yet couldn't. It was one thing to fight when someone suddenly came at you. It was another to worry about it all morning and into the afternoon like a fighter going into the ring. Elizabeth had doubtless been trying to be helpful in telling him the time. But it was grating on him now like a dull razor cutting across his nerves.

Suddenly the door whooshed open and this time four guards stood at the entrance. One handed him a muzzle.

"Put it on the dog, now." He motioned with his 9mm, slamming the barrel into Stone's stomach, who didn't appreciate the gesture at all and got a good look at the bastard's face, hoping they'd meet up again under better circumstances. Stone put the muzzle around Excaliber's mouth, who pulled back from the thing. The dog hated being muzzled but he allowed Stone to proceed, knowing somehow he had to for some weird human reason. With the muzzle on, the guards led Stone and the mutt down the long corridor to the far end of the level and the elevator banks. Stone tried to memorize everything and fit it into the schematic that he had spent hours going over all afternoon until he felt like it was drilled into his head. It better be if he got the chance to test it out. One wrong turn in this twisting puzzle of corridors and seamless walls and he'd be as lost as a retarded rat in a maze.

They took them down two levels in a wide freight elevator and then marched out again down the corridor. Two immense black steel doors were already pulled back and Stone was led inside. It was the biggest of all the chambers he'd been in since being underground. Not just wide, but high too, going up nearly sixty feet. On all four sides of the hundred foot square beginning about twenty feet up were rows of seats behind thick bulletproof glass. Stone suddenly got the message. This was the football of the psycho set. The Dwarf and his pals kept their underlings happy with a little controlled blood letting. So he was Superbowl Sunday—him and the dog. He scouted around and saw the ten freaks, staring down at him through tinted blue glass. They were in good moods, drinking and laughing, gesticulating with their claws and stumps. Stone saw the Dwarf among them, staring down. He wasn't moving but just still as a rock as if in a trance. Across the floor from the ten were the rest of the military crew, rows of greenshirts all jumping around behind their glass partitions. They were usually subdued and businesslike around the subterranean headquarters, but here they were allowed to let it all hang out. And they where whooping it up, screaming for his blood. Stone had a lot of fans out there.

"I think they like us," he lied to the pit bull after the guards had pulled back and the wall was once again as flat as a sheet of glass around the entire square. Stone felt for the icepick rigged up with some thread he had taken from his slacks and wrapped around the thing. It was hanging loosely so he could whip forward with his hand and it would slide right into his palm, then back again if he reversed the flicking motion of the wrist. Or so it had worked in the cell. Out here facing God knew what was something else. Stone made a quick onceover of the place but didn't see a single opening or crack in the lining.

Then he heard the low hum of the pneumatic systems of the main Games door operating and a ten foot section of the arena pulled back. There was just darkness on the other side and Stone strained his eyes to see as he pulled back instinctively. Then he saw them, darting forward into the bright light cast down from dozens of spots above. Two mastiffs, the largest of the species he'd ever seen. They could have been the brothers of the Hound of the Baskervilles, standing a good five feet at the shoulders. Stone estimated their weight at two-fifty plus, more like small lions than dogs. Even Excaliber made a low sound that got caught in his throat and stepped behind Stone like a kid behind his older brother when the neighborhood gang shows up. Only Stone had the same idea about the dog.

The crowds above cheered wildly and Stone could hear them even through the two inch thick Plexiglas. The mastiffs slowed down as they trotted around to see just what the hell was going on. Even dinosaur-sized dogs with teeth that could have done construction work liked to check out the situation. And seeing what it was, they both seemed to laugh canine-style, snorting up a storm and bumping into each other as they jumped around in some sort of ritual dance. Stone got the feeling they'd done this sort of thing before, which didn't encourage him greatly.

The pit bull growled at his heels as it kept looking up at Stone, wanting to know what the plan was as the two monsters pawed at the cement preparing to make their move. But Stone had no plan. Or he thought he had no plan until the mastiffs, who looked like they should have been guarding the royal tomb at Thebes, came charging from across the floor. Then Stone turned and ran like a sprinter, with the pit bull right at his heels. With some firepower it would be a different story. But the dogs didn't seem like they would be open to any sympathetic pleadings to let him go out and buy a few. Stone tore straight to the far wall until he was about ten feet away. At the last second he turned and saw the right hand mastiff just yards behind him and ready to leap. He slowed slightly and let the thing get right up to him, sensing just when it was going to leave the floor.

Just as Stone was about to slam right into the wall he suddenly threw himself down to the cement, taking a hard hit on his shoulder. But the mastiff, which had launched itself at his head, took an even harder hit as its own head slammed into the wall of steel at about thirty miles an hour. The mastiff came sliding down the side of the wall on top of Stone but was too spaced out to do more than make sputtering sounds and quiver. Stone pushed with all his might and slid out from beneath the oppressive weight. As he came to his feet he heard a terrible yowling a few yards away and saw Excaliber and the other mastiff, this one with a gold coat almost like a lion's, going at it hot and heavy. At least the mastiff was trying to go at it but the pit bull with its penchant for tactics and fucking with the other animal's head had grabbed hold of the canine's back left paw and kept dragging it backwards. The mastiff was hopping around like a kangaroo who'd drunk Super Test, unable to get a good footing and stop itself from being dragged, no matter what it did. Of course once Excaliber stopped he was in a shitload of trouble. But he wasn't thinking about stopping.

Suddenly Stone heard a fierce growling from just behind him and turned to see that the knocked-out mastiff who had been on his ass seconds before wasn't knocked out anymore. Its eyes were focused and it was up on all fours, pointing its teeth at him like a hundred spears ready to enter flesh. Stone rushed a few feet off, sliding along the wall as he shook his right hand with the icepick in it, and it flew up into his palm. He was proud of himself, the contraption worked like a charm. Now he just had to make like a bullfighter and lure the dog toward him, make it jump at exactly the right angle.

Just as it leaped into the air straight at his face Stone stepped to the side away from the wall. Snapping out with the icepick but hiding the handle completely so it couldn't be seen from the peanut gallery above, he ripped it toward the dog's face with the same speed that it was coming up. Its jaws opened and closed at the hand but missed and the tip of the icepick slid right into the corner of the dog's left eye, all the way to the hilt. Stone heard a sharp squeal and then ripped the pick back out again, hiding it beneath the sleeve as the dog sailed past. It came down cold stone dead, hitting the floor on its tail and sliding along like it had a stick of butter up its ass. It came to a stop about fifteen feet away with a trickle of red sliding out of its eye and over the golden face.

Above him Stone saw a commotion as some of the crowd were screaming that he was using a weapon. But the Dwarf didn't budge from his death trance as he stared down. Stone would get to keep the icepick. Stone turned and sighted up the pit bull, who was just about losing it with the paw and pull contest. Suddenly the mastiff threw itself down onto its side, ripping the foot free with all its might. The great momentum of the mastiff put too great a strain on the tendons and bone of such a mighty dog, for the pit bull didn't let go an inch, but tightened its jaws just as the mastiff spun over. The huge dog's whole right paw and about four inches of leg came off in the pit bull's mouth. Excaliber fell backwards as it had been pulling so hard.

The mastiff let out a howl of mortal pain that seemed to thrill the crowd above and made them forget about Stone's illegal weapon. He saw his chance and while the mastiff was dragging itself along on three legs plus a bloody stump that left a trail of sticky red behind it as it hobbled after the pit bull, Stone snuck up behind it. Excaliber sensed what Stone had in mind and lured the mastiff on, keeping just out of its range. The killer kept lunging forward, but it was in pitiful shape now with just three legs, not even able to judge quite how to walk anymore. Stone dove through the air as he saw the dog's attention was fully focused on the pit bull. He came down on the creature's back and stabbed the ice pick into the center of its skull. The sharp point of the pick sank cleanly in like a knife into butter and Stone pushed with all his might until he couldn't push any further. Then he twisted and turned it all around like an Italian mother stirring a spaghetti sauce.

The mastiff struggled violently, trying to snap at Stone's hand. But the pit bull charged in and grabbed it around the throat, holding it down while Stone ripped the pick free and then sank it in again—and again. In a few more seconds it was over. Blood covered the floor for yards around as the animal's skull had fractured in places and was oozing red from fissures in the bone. Stone stood up as the crowd above booed and stomped angrily. He bowed first to them and then to the Dwarf. The Dwarf's mouth was set into a fixed cheshire cat of a smile, and he nodded slowly. Behind him, Stone heard the door opening.

Nineteen

IF Stone had thought the Tribunal of Ten not to be the greatest looking guys, the two men walking out of the darkness of the tunnel were nightmares. Besides the fact that they were seven feet tall plus a few inches and had arms that should have had leaves on them and been in the ground—they both had extra appendages. One a third arm coming out of the center of its chest, and the other an extra leg that came out behind it at the base of the spine. All the extra baggage seemed to be in perfect working condition as far as Stone could see as the two strode in. Not that they needed it, but each had weapons in addition to his innate bull strength. The three-legged one carried a long sword that must have run six feet from stem to stern and a car door sized shield, while the three-armed one carried two machete-like blades and a net in the extra hand. All in all, between them they looked like it would take a whole division to subdue them. But Stone looked around and saw only himself and the dog.

As he had done with the mastiffs he pulled back as far away as he could from the two mutant men. They were known to the crowd, for when they raised their arms to the glass screens above the greenshirts went wild. Mickey Mantle, Wilt Chamberlain and Joe Namath all rolled up into two hunks of overmuscled flesh. At last when they'd had enough of their strutting and preening for the masses, they hefted their weapons and set out to take care of business. Stone and the dog reached the far wall and there was nowhere else to go. As the two reconstituted fighters came tearing ass across the cement floor Stone pushed Excaliber in the opposite direction from him along the wall.

"Run boy, let's split them in two—keep moving. Go!" The pit bull looked at the two rolling mountains coming their way and took off along the steel wall moving like a rocket. Stone ripped off the other way pumping his legs as fast as they would carry him. Both of them just got the angle right so the two NAUASC fighters came barreling right by them. Both men having such mass took yards to stop and nearly slammed into the wall. It took them a full ten seconds to get themselves all rearranged and set for a charge again. It was like fighting elephants rather than men. But on the other hand Stone could use their great momentum and long stopping time to his advantage.

He halted when he reached the far wall and saw Excaliber already there waiting for him, tongue huffing and almond eyes looking up asking what the hell next, Chow Boy? Only Chow Boy had nothing more to offer than what he had just done. Run—and try to sneak a sucker punch in on the bastard.

"Split up again, dog—meet you on the other side." He waited until the two giants were halfway across again, sword and machetes spinning in the air, then Stone screamed "Go!" and they both took off. He started right along the wall again knowing the three-legged one would think he was going to go the same way he had a minute before. The mutation changed his angle, heading to cut Stone off at the pass, but the would-be victim altered his own course with the turn of an ankle and shot by on the inside of the flailing bruiser. As he crouched down the giant's long sword flew by right above him. Stone ripped the icepick from his sleeve and stabbed it hard into the thing's leg. He had been aiming for thigh muscle, but hit the kneecap, which was just fine with Stone. As the man mountain flew by Stone ripped the pick out again and then ran forward all the way back to the wall as the three-armer let out a howl of pain and had to slow down a little as its right leg started looking a little wobbly.

"All right," Stone hissed under his breath as he ran. He had actually hurt the bastard. As he turned his head away for a few seconds, knowing it was going to take a little time for the big fellow to get his act together, Stone saw that the three-armer was having his own devil of a time really getting a handle on the pit bull too. It seemed like the dog was always just within reach of his two machetes and suddenly it was gone. Twice he threw the net and missed completely as the dog almost seemed to mock him, trying to get him angry. But on the third throw of the net the dog misjudged slightly and got its hindquarters caught in the thin steel mesh. The three-armed fighter came in for the kill, slamming down both machetes toward the canine as if ready to skewer it for the cooking fire. Somehow the dog flew up from the concrete trying to out-race the descending steel blades. He did, just barely. As both two-foot-long blades ripped down the pit bull flew in under them and straight up into the face of the three-armer. He snapped hold around the giant's lower face, sinking canines deep into already twisted cheek and mouth and nose tissue.

Still, even mutant giants don't like having their faces turned into bloodburgers. The three-armed fighter flailed up at the dog and managed to slash it hard right along the neck. The animal dropped the hold sensing a second strike and rolled over backwards a few times, spinning out a spiral of blood as it flew.

"Oh Christ," Stone muttered, his stomach dropping down to his knees. But the dog hit the ground and was moving fast. Stone saw that the blood flow was bad but not fatal—not yet. But his momentary distraction by the dog's actions had made him forget for a few seconds that the other one was still kicking. And he had gotten himself going a little quicker than Stone expected, for suddenly

there was a whistling sound coming straight at his head and
Stone, pulling back as he turned to see what it was, sighted
the three-legger's sword coming posthaste. The split-second
warning enabled him to pull back from the blow—but
only partially. The edge of the sword slid into the side of
his chest. It sliced down across three or four ribs leaving a
half inch deep gash before the blade continued past him
and cracked into the concrete floor, sending sparks flying
everywhere.

Stone waited a fraction of a second to see if he was dead
or alive. Discovering that he was still standing, he shot off
sideways and managed to just avoid the back thrust of the
blade. Now he'd definitely gotten the sucker mad and
three-leg came tearing at him, hobbling along on the ice-
picked knee. Stone walked quickly backwards as if in a
walking race in the wrong direction. He didn't want to take
his eyes off the killer a second time. There wouldn't be a
third. He heard a dreadful howl and didn't know if it was
Excaliber or the three-armer. And he sure as hell didn't
have time to look.

Suddenly his back was against the wall and the thing
was there like a charging rhino. Stone barely managed to
sidestep the blow but even as he ripped out to do some
damage with the pick, the third leg, which he had somehow forgotten about, came flying up. It was aimed at his
testicles, but Stone was able to pull his thigh around to take
the blow. The power of the kick sent him slamming into
the metal wall and then bouncing right off it and past the
giant. Stone was unconscious for a fraction of a second but
made himself come to fast. Even his unconscious knew
there was no time to play games.

The three-legged fighter came out swinging the sword
with one hand and waving the immense chromium shield
with the other, trying to hypnotize Stone with the reflec-
tions that bounced off the thing. And it was almost working. Stone had to shield his eyes as he moved away, having
a hard time getting a clear view. Suddenly the sword was
descending and as he shot away the shield came down like

a guillotine and hit him square in the chest. He went down like the lights were going out for good and just barely managed to hang on. As he hit the cold hard floor Stone fell onto his side. He looked up through pain-dazed eyes and saw the giant looming above him like he extended up into the ceiling. The man was savoring his moment of triumph as Stone lay at his feet. He raised his sword up for the crowd's approval, making them scream for him to begin the final descent. Only his PR stunt cost him too much time. Stone's head cleared, enough to know that his nose was about an inch away from the dude's huge smelly boot. Stone without even thinking about it ripped the ice-pick from his sleeve and slammed it straight into the top of the leather boot. It slid easily through the hide and down into the bone and then right through the foot.

The three-legged fighter let out a howl and ripped up his middle foot in agony. As the leg came up Stone pulled the icepick out and rolled onto his back. Before the killer could move an inch he thrust the icepick right up into the thing's groin, pushing with everything he had. If the howl before had been loud, this one was thunderous. The man mountain jumped backwards, throwing his sword and shield to the floor as he grabbed at his torn genitalia. He screamed as he bounced backward like a yo-yo gone haywire until he slammed into the wall. He fell there on his side like a beached whale and made mewing sounds as his whole body went into shock.

Stone tore his attention back behind him where he held one of the strangest things he'd ever seen. The pit bull had somehow gotten the three-armed one in a clamp bite around one ear. But the man was holding the pit bull in the air a good six feet off the ground with two of its three arms. Yet it couldn't throw the dog or the whole ear would come off. The third arm was reaching around for the ma-chete it had dropped on the ground when the dog had taken half of his face off. Stone reached down and hefted the immense sword the three-legger had dropped. It was hard to even carry as it must have weighed eighty pounds plus, not exactly ideal weight for a sword. Stone gripped the thing with both hands and tore as fast as his shaking legs could carry him across the bloody arena.

Three-arms had just found his blade and was about to bring it up into the pit bull's guts when Stone's blunderbuss of steel sliced down right at the elbow. The third arm fell from the mutation's chest and dropped to the ground where it lay there spasming, the fingers opening and closing around the handle ·of the weapon. Suddenly three-arm decided he didn't give a shit about his ear after all and heaved the dog with all his might back against the wall. Excaliber went soaring a good nine feet off the ground, ear and all in his mouth, trailing bloody tendrils and veins. The giant turned toward Stone with red cascading down the side of his face. He was so pissed off now he seemed oblivious to the pain, and with a roar worthy of King Kong on a bad night, he leaped at Stone who, not being prepared for such speed and anger, didn't have time to bring the sword up again.

Before he knew it the weapon was flying from his hands and both remaining arms of the beastman were around him. The thing lifted him in a bear hug, the ripped ugly face only inches from his own. The breath alone made Stone want to surrender. But it was his own breath he was more concerned about as it was being squeezed out of him as if in the grip of a python. There was no way in hell he could break the hold. Stone could feel the vertebrae along his back bending in and threatening to crack in the not too distant future as the pressure grew tremendous.

Stone felt something digging hard into his neck. He reached over and touched the pen gun that he'd bought. It was a gun—you just had to turn it. Turn it, turn it! His brain was already going out from lack of oxygen, everything gray and strange with a blue outline around it all. Stone knew he had less than a second or two. He lifted his hand up so the tip of the mini-gun slammed right up against the mess of scarred flesh that was the forehead. Then he turned the thing hard.

There was a sharp crack, and for a second or two the arms didn't release around him but seemed to grow even tighter. Stone slipped into blackness for an instant. But just as quickly the arms loosened slowly like a mother releasing her child against her will. Stone's eyes opened and he saw a tiny red hole dead center of the giant's head with pink stuff leaking out of front and back. Then the arms fell away completely and the fighter staggered backwards, did a pirouette and then fell over, slamming his face into a pulp as he hit the concrete. He never felt it.

Stone wearily picked himself up off the floor and took a look over at three-legs. He wasn't doing too hot either. He didn't seem to be exactly dead, but just rolling around on the floor making sounds like a hyena in heat. Stone walked over to Excaliber, who was sitting bone-tired with a little pool of blood collecting below his chest where the sliced neck was still flowing freely. The dog's eyes were bright and as Stone approached it, it looked up at him and managed a weak bark as if to say, "We kicked bukanky today, Chow Boy, and I'll be expecting something special tonight on the dinner table." Stone didn't have the heart to tell the dog that if he knew the Dwarf at all there was a fair chance they wouldn't be having dinner at all tonight. They wouldn't be having dinner ever.

Twenty

STONE stood in the center of the steel-walled arena with the dead lying around him and raised his fist up at the Dwarf.

"I won, now give me my fucking sister and let me out of here." The Dwarf at last came out of his trance, his eyes opening wide, his stumps starting to move around frantically like they always did when he was thinking hard.

"I never said you would win anything," the eggman laughed into a microphone in front of him so that his voice echoed throughout the metal room. "That was in your own mind. But I must say that I'm not all that surprised that you won. I've always known you were my greatest adversary since the first time we met. And in a way, I'm actually pleased. For now you can attend my wedding, be my best man—as I'd hoped. After all, I want to give the blushing bride away, Stone. It will be the core of the ceremony."

Stone rushed at the wall in a maddened rage and tried to scale its seamless side. It was ridiculous, he couldn't get up higher than he could jump and then just drop down again. High above the Dwarf stabbed at the buttons of his wheelchair and the motorized war machine turned and headed out. He motioned for his underlings who milled around him like bees to get Stone prepared. Below, Stone walked back to the dog just as the door slid open and four greenshirts came in. But Stone was in no mood for any more bullshit. He reached down and grabbed hold of one of the dead fighter's machetes and hefted it in his hand.

"Okay assholes, who's first?" he snarled as they came up to him in a semicircle.

"You," the head man smirked and whipped up a can of something. He sprayed it right into Stone's face, who headed into bye-bye land before he could even get off a single blow. He saw the steel floor coming up at him fast and then—darkness.

When he came to God knew how many hours later he was instantly inundated with sound and light. Stone opened his eyes, wincing as the bright light was painful. His head throbbed badly and it was hard to see anything at first. Then he did. The Dwarf was up on a platform—with April sitting just a few feet away from him with the same dazed expression she'd had the last time he saw her. The Dwarf was decked out in full tuxedo, with the arms and legs cut off so his stumps poked through. April was dressed in— Stone could hardly bear to look. It was obscene—the virginal white wedding gown that had been turned into a mockery of the institution of marriage with the chest cut open so both her breasts were pushing out. And the same around her pelvic area, and Stone was sure—the backside as well. The guy was a real joker.

Stone stifled the impulse to start screaming his lungs out as it hadn't done too much good the last few times other than hurt his throat. He was in the Tribunal Chamber, only instead of its dark and judgmental tones, it was lit up and decorated with streamers and ornaments all over the walls. The rest of the freaks sat in various chairs and couches in a circle around the stage which had been erected for the event. Tables were filled with food and drink, the usual retinue of unclothed and semi-clothed women were there. Stone was clearly in the "in" crowd. He looked down and saw that he was wearing a tux as well. They'd stripped him down and gotten him totally reclothed in full wedding regalia. And he was strapped as usual to a metal chair:

feet, arms, chest, everything. He couldn't move an inch, other than his head.

"Ah, Stone," the Dwarf said from the platform as he turned away from gazing on the stoned beauty of April, who gazed ahead, clearly on another planet.

"Dwarf, you're not really going through with this—wedding, are you?" Stone asked, knowing full well the answer, but not being able to stomach it.

"Go through with it?" the Dwarf shrieked. "We've been waiting for you to become conscious, they gave you a little too much gas. Why look, half my guests are already asleep." Stone saw that indeed six of the freaks were already stoned out of their minds, lying in their recliners with mouths open and drool and slime dripping on everything.

"And now you are back among the living, so we may proceed. Priest, please," the Dwarf motioned. A frazzled-looking old man with hair white as snow all tousled up on top of his head came stumbling out from behind a curtain. He wore a religious frock, only this one had studs, obscene writing and graffiti all over it. The "priest" looked at the Dwarf and appeared about ready to faint.

"What's wrong, padre?" the Dwarf asked, standing tall on his stumps in the wheelchair. "You look tired."

"Sorry, Mr. Dwarf, I'm not feeling well—the trip from Colbranch was hard and long. We were attacked and—"

"My men did not treat you well?" the Dwarf asked, the color starting to redden in his corpse-like pasty cheeks.

"Oh no, Mr. Dwarf, I mean yes, Mr. Dwarf," the priest stuttered, terrified by the eggman and the rest of the freaks. "They treated me very well, very well."

"Good, good," Dwarf said. "Then we may begin. Now, first you definitely are a priest, I mean ordained and all that?" Dwarf asked.

"Well, I was once, before the collapse and—"

"Before the collapse, that's all I want to know," the Dwarf said. "That in the eyes of the dead laws of the U.S. means that it's all legal. For my forebears will rule and I don't want any problems with any contenders challenging the legality of my marriage or the birth of my children down the line. You understand?"

"Uh yes, I—understand. So you're going to mar-ry the girl sitting here?" the priest asked, hardly able to believe his eyes. Why had he let the slime talk him into coming? The money they had offered—twenty pieces of silver. It was a fortune. But now it hardly seemed enough.

"Yes I'm going to marry the girl," the Dwarf shrieked back. "Any problems with that? Who the hell else did you think was going to marry her?"

"Oh sorry, sorry, sorry Mr. Dwarf." The priest looked around to see just what his chances were of fleeing right out of the place. None. Guards stood at every wall, in full honor guard at the Dwarf's wedding. He was here for the duration. The priest suddenly smiled his widest, most forced fake smile at the Dwarf, an expression he had used successfully many times before in dealing with the general public.

"Ah good, good, now everything is all straightened out, is it?" the Dwarf laughed, motioning with his right stump for an underling to hand the priest some papers. "These are the words you will read," the Dwarf said. "And then I will give her this ring." He held up an immense diamond between his two stumps and spun it around. The priest pitied the poor girl sitting there drugged like a zombie. But he wasn't going to sacrifice his life. There was nothing he could do.

"Yes of course," the priest said, taking the papers. He took out some spectacles from his chest pocket and put them on, reading the words down the page. "Oh, I don't think—"

"Of course you can," the Dwarf said quickly. "Of course you can. Not let's get on with it."

"I . . . I . . ." the priest's hand shook, holding the paper in it. He still believed somewhere inside of him in God, even though he was a charlatan. It frightened him in his very soul to commit the sacrilege that the Dwarf wanted him to by reading the blasphemous words. The Dwarf motioned with his head and one of his elite bodyguards who were always near him walked the two yards to the priest, who stood in the middle of the stage and held his 9mm up against the man's temple. He took off the safety with a loud click. The priest gulped hard, his Adam's apple bobbing up and down like a plumber's plunger.

"All right, I'll do it, I'll do it," he choked out, seeing his wife and children dead without him—or very happy with the twenty silver pieces he would bring home. Conscience could only go so far in the new world.

"Good. Excellent," the Dwarf said, holding out his stump. "Hold my hand, dear," he smiled sweetly at April, whose head turned slowly like a robot, on rusty gears.

"Yes dear, I will hold your hand," she echoed, reaching out and taking hold of the purple red stump. Then she turned her head back again, looking straight ahead.

"Dearly ugly and diseased," the priest began, halting on every word that came from his mouth. "We are gathered here today to give Dwarf a breeding bitch. One who will bring him a boy child into this world who will someday rule over all the lands, from sea to burning sea." The Dwarf had a wide smile on his squashed face and Stone suddenly started screaming again in spite of himself. He couldn't stand to see this happening. It was worse than his worse nightmare. He had failed her, had failed his whole family. And now was being forced to watch the final humiliation. But even as he screamed and the priest stopped and looked up startled, one of the greenshirts rushed over and slammed a gag around Stone's mouth, cutting the sound off.

Once order had been restored the priest continued on. "Let it hereforth be known that April Stone shall have two years to produce a freak man child. All female children shall be destroyed at birth. As will all normal male children. Only a freak boy like Dwarf himself shall live. He shall be the Dwarf's only legitimate offspring with there being no other claims to the leadership of the NAUASC council." The Dwarf's smile seemed to grow even wider as he sat in his wheelchair like the cat who had just swallowed the rat. "If April Stone does not produce the required freak child, this marriage shall be considered null and void and Dwarf shall be free to choose another breeding bitch."

The priest paused and seemed to look up at the metal ceiling as if begging God for forgiveness for his reading of the black ceremony. But he went on.

"And now—will the bride please recite the following words."

"Dear," the Dwarf said, shaking his stump within her hand. "The man wants you to say some words."

"Yes, I shall say some words," she said, turning toward the priest with a dead expression.

"I, April Stone do hereby swear—"

"I, April Stone do hereby square," she said, not quite getting it right as she slurred her words from the effects of the tranquilizer that had been pumped into her for two weeks now.

"To serve the Dwarf and only the Dwarf."

"To serve the Dwarf and honly the Dwarf."

"And carry out his every command, even the death of my own child."

"And carry out his every rommand, even the death of my own ch-hild."

"And do all that I can to make the Dwarf satisfied."

"And do all that I can to make the Dwarf sad is filed."

"And I, Dwarf," the priest said, turning to the armless, legless monster.

"And I, Dwarf."

"Promise to protect and obey April Stone from all others who would try to use her ovaries for reproductive purposes."

"Promise to protect April Stone from all others who try to use her ovaries for reproductive purposes," the Dwarf replied, looking with lovesick eyes into the dilated pupils of April.

"And I promise to give her a full two years to produce a freak boy child."

"And shall give her a full two years to produce a freak boy child."

"I now—pronounce you," the priest said, going slower and slower as if he couldn't stand to say the final words on the page. "Man and—wife. You may ki—kk-kkiss the bride." The priest let his hand holding the paper fall to his side and his head fell down to his chest with a look of utter shame.

The Dwarf leaned over in the wheelchair and held out his puckered white lips. Stone felt himself gag but held it all back as he knew if he puked with a cloth around his mouth, he'd drown in the stuff. April turned her face under the Dwarf's hypnotic gaze and will and their lips met. Stone could see the Dwarf's little reptile-like tongue digging around to get between her lips, but she was so drugged out that her teeth remained closed as she stared straight at the Dwarf's forehead. She didn't know where she was; this was some consolation for her. But not for Martin Stone, who struggled furiously within his bounds, not even caring that he was ripping his legs and arms and wrists to shreds against the metal cables that held him down.

"Come," the Dwarf said, pulling his face back from his bride's and sweeping his stump around the room. "Time to eat and drink. Time to celebrate the greatest moment of the twentieth century—and the woman who shall bear the future emperor of the world."

CHAPTER

Twenty-one

WHEN all the smooching had been done and toasts raised, Dwarf poked at the panel of his wheelchair with April walking alongside him, her hand resting on the back rest of the chair. The eggman headed off the pre-fab stage and down a ramp along one side to join his fellow freaks. They were sloshing down everything in sight into misshapen mouths, scaled and burned hands squeezing tight on glasses and young breasts. The priest remained standing there alone on the stage not sure what he was supposed to do next. He could hardly bear to look at the mob of freaks below him or at the woman he had just hitched to the mini-monster.

"Priestie," the Dwarf shouted up from the floor below. "It was decreed in my dream vision that the priest who married me to my anointed one was not to ever perform another ceremony. This is to be the last." The priest got a nervous look on his already heavily sweating face.

"You mean I can't perform marriages, or funerals or—"

"Exactly," the Dwarf said, letting a nasty smile dance across his face. Stone, who watched it all from across the room, had never seen the Dwarf so happy. Clearly, marrying his sister had done wonders for the monster's mood. "And though I'm sure you could promise me that you wouldn't—and you might even try not to," the Dwarf went

on, "somewhere along the line you would fail, being only
human like all of us. Therefore," the eggman continued as
he leaned over in the wheelchair and poised him left stump
above a red button, "although I surely do appreciate the
long distance and the many dangers you underwent to get
here—I must terminate you. Goodbye." The goodbye was
said almost sweetly, for the Dwarf did appreciate this day,
would always remember it and treasure it in his heart. But
the dream demanded it.

He stabbed down at the button and a great white arc of
electricity shot down from the ceiling and ripped through
the priest's head, down through his body and into the floor.
Stone's eyes grew wide, and for the first time in the last
hour he stopped struggling within the steel chair as he
watched the bolts of megawatts rip into the body. The man
was instantly dancing around wildly like a puppet attached
to a jackhammer. His mouth was horribly contorted in a
wide scream but no sound came out as his arms flung out
and around like a boxer who can't decide what to hit.

But he only pogo-sticked around for about ten seconds.
Then plumes of smoke began rising up from his mouth and
ears, all the orifices of his body, thick and nauseating, filling the air above him with a cloud of his own smoldering
flesh. Suddenly flames appeared all over him and the priest
continued to dance around, only on fire now. Within seconds every square inch of him was rippling with blue
flames. Even the electric chair didn't burn its occupants
into something left in a broiler all afternoon.

The flaming thing just kept burning and lurching around
a few square feet, unable to escape the clutching pull of the
supercurrent. It burned until there was nothing to consume
anymore and then the charred bones of the corpse crumbled
like old charcoal down onto the floor. The electric bolts
shot into the pile of what had been a man for another few
seconds, grinding even that up into finer dust. When Dwarf
pushed his stump at the off button there was nothing left
except an ink black powder almost as fine as sand spread

out all around the stage atop a burnt rug, which had covered the steel plating beneath.

The other freaks applauded and lauded the Dwarf from out of their drunkenness, screaming out their compliments at the afternoon's entertainment. Once again the Dwarf hadn't failed them. Stone glared at the eggman through itching eyes as some of the smoke of the dead man had wafted into his face and irritated his eyes, which were watering up like little geysers now.

The festivities went on for nearly four hours. The Dwarf left the dust on the stage, feeling it was part of the day's aesthetic. At last as nearly all of the freaks had passed out or vomited so many times that they had to be taken off to the medical section, Dwarf appeared to tire as well.

"Well, I guess that even the happiest of occasions must end," he said, addressing the assemblage though only two of the freaks were still there or able to listen, and they waved glasses back and forth in front of their hideous faces. "So adieu, adieu old friends and now I shall retire with—my bride."

"Yeah," a reptile face screamed out, throwing his scaled hand down over his groin area. "Give it to her good, Dwarf. Make her scream."

"Oh, you'll be hearing us tonight," the jaundice-faced groom said, throwing his brandy glass toward the stage and the still smoldering ashes of the priest. He flung it with both stumps like a seal trying to dump a rotten fish. It flew out from the purple appendages only a foot or so where it smashed into pieces on the concrete. "Come dear," he said slurring as he leaned over and addressed April. "Let us retire to our—honeymoon suite."

"Yes—our honeymoon," April echoed as she walked along behind the Dwarf, who aimed his chair toward one of the exits, where his private elevator was waiting to whisk them to his full-level living quarters.

"What about Stone?" his chief of internal security asked as Dwarf passed him at the door.

"I've no more need for him," the Dwarf hiccupped

drunkenly. "Give him to Dr. Kerhausen, he wants him for some crazy experiment." Then the Dwarf was gone from Stone's view—and his sister as well.

"Come on scum, it's the end of the road for you," a greenshirt said pushing the chair, which had wheels beneath it, along down the corridor. He chuckled as he wheeled it, apparently amused by the day's events—and what was about to befall Stone. "He's a brilliant man, Dr. Kerhausen is," the greenshirt said. "You're going to be a very lucky man to be part of such a—" Again he began laughing, and then managed to sputter out the words, "medical experiment." He wheeled Stone into one of the freight elevators and then up several levels and into the doctor's medical facilities.

Stone could see straight ahead, and he didn't like this room at all—with men cut up and sewn together again lying on stretchers all over the place like discarded dolls. Then he saw an empty operating table with equipment all around it, and life support machines beeping. Two medical techs were standing by with white gowns already on. And next to the bed—already unconscious and strapped down to a second table—was Excaliber. Stone's eyes really filled with tears now. Had they had already killed the dog? It wasn't moving at all.

"Here, here now," Dr. Kerhausen said as he stepped from behind a blinking contraption. "I told you we would meet again, that our fates were intertwined. And that time is now. I want you to know that I am honored to share this moment with you and shall always think fondly of you." Stone sputtered but with a gag in his mouth not a hell of a lot came out.

"Yes, yes, I know you have so much to say before you go. But unfortunately there is no time for words, just for cutting. All the facilities are ready. Let us begin." Dr. Kerhausen tied on his surgical gown and then slid on rubber gloves. As he put them on, two of the dozen gowned assistants took Stone's chair and fiddled with it. Stone prepared himself to come out fighting were there the slightest opportunity. But they didn't give him one, pushing a button so the chair straightened out flat beneath him and then lifting it up onto the operating table with him now stretched out on it. And for the first time Stone had to really be honest with himself—that there was no way out. He couldn't do a fucking thing to stop this maniac from cutting him to ribbons. Two of them began slicing his clothes right from his body, careful not to cut the skin. Within seconds he was stark naked on the table and shivering with cold metal beneath his back and legs.

"Is the video camera and the recorder on?" Kerhausen asked one of the already masked assistants who stood waiting around the table. "I want this to be recorded for all posterity—no hitches. This operation will be as history making—as the Wright Brothers flight. For with men and beasts mixed together as one, new kinds of workers will be able to be created. Man/Beasts with the intelligence of homo sapiens—but the brute strength of the animal." He was ranting louder as if acting out a scene in front of an audience of thousands. The video was checked several times, camera mounted on a clamp on the ceiling looking straight down so it could note every little slice.

"Take off his gag," Dr. Kerhausen said, donning his own mask. "He needs full breathing facilities—or it will kill him." One of the assistants cut the gag from Stone's mouth with a scalpel and it fell away. "Now you can scream all you want Mr. Stone," Kerhausen said softly. "Down here—it is fine to scream. Your anger will oxygenate your blood, it will give you strength to survive."

"Survive what?" Stone asked, "the mutilation of me and my dog?"

"Mutilation—oh no, something far above that. It's true we shall cut off pieces of your dog—but only to reattach them to you. And take your pieces—and put them on the animal. It is really quite a daring undertaking."

"Jesus God," Stone muttered under his breath. "You and Hitler must have been great friends," he snarled.

"Oh, we had our moments," Kerhausen laughed from within his operating mask. "What I wouldn't give to have his body here now. I know I could resurrect him, clone him somehow. Ah—but that is not to be. So I must settle for the first dog-man."

"Now gather around," Dr. Kerhausen said, cutting off Stone's talking as his assistants all came in close around the table Stone was lying on. The doctor took a magic marker and began drawing along Stone's shoulder all the way around, then at the top of both thighs. "We shall cut here," he said. "I want to give him the dog's legs—but keep one human arm. It will be interesting to see the advantages of having such a mixture. Quite interesting."

While they drew their lines and circles and made sure everyone understood just what their function would be in the complex four-hour double back-and-forth transplant— with a second team working just on the dog. Stone managed to turn his head a few inches the other way to see what was on the far side. Kerhausen's last experiment, the half man/half woman. It didn't look like it was doing too good, with both breasts that had been sewn onto its chest rotting right off so that bone was exposed beneath. One of its arms was much smaller than the other, but that too was shriveling up, turning a deep purple and green color, giving off a foul odor. Stone felt himself shudder deep inside for he was about to become something like that—worse. And as he looked at the pain-wracked face, the eyes opened and caught Stone unprepared.

"Kill me," the lips mouthed silently, though not a word came out. "Please kill me." The mouth and lips of a woman had been transplanted as well, and not very well, so two small fleshy lines barely covered the teeth, giving the whole face a skeletal smile. Stone ripped his head away, unable to look at the pitiful creature. Never had he felt so alone, so desperate. If only he could have gone down fighting, shooting, punching, anything. He had expected to go out that way. And in a dark way had been prepared for it. But not this, not like this, oh please God not like this.

"Scalpel, nurse," Dr. Kerhausen said, holding his gloved hand out.

CHAPTER
Twenty-two

S TONE felt the scalpel just start to cut into his
shoulder right along the dotted line when there was
suddenly a thunderous roar at the far end of the medical
level. All motion stopped in its tracks and Dr. Kerhausen
held the scalpel just fractions of an inch above Stone's
flesh, listening as they were all dead silent. For just a second or two there was nothing and the good doctor dug the
tip of the bade back into the flesh thinking it was some
accident out in the freight elevator—someone else's problem not his. Suddenly there was another roar and this time
a flash of light and smoke just a few rooms down.

"Get the patients out of here," Kerhausen screamed out,
giving Stone a look of utter rage that his historic operation
had been momentarily thwarted. The nurses and orderlies
had just begun to disconnect Stone and the dog when there
was the roar of engines and to Stone's amazement a whole
slew of motorcycles came riding right down the corridor
from the next set of operating rooms. They came ahead like
nothing could stop them, riding over tables, sending chairs
and anyone who got in their flying. Suddenly he saw them
clearly. It was the Ballbusters, the female biker gang who he
had barely escaped from. What the hell were they . . . ?
But his musings didn't have a chance to get any further

as Raspberry Thorn ripped up a sawed-off SMG and sprayed the orderlies shooting out a full burst at chest level. The others on each side of her opened up as well as bodies went rocketing everywhere, cut apart like they had cut others apart, arms, ears, eyes flying off. More bikes screeched to a stop and more operating tables went flying, including a few corpses that the doctor had brought in.

"Jesus Christ," Stone said as Raspberry got off her bike, letting it go on a few more feet, slamming into a wall of surgical gear which went exploding out onto the floor. "What the hell are you doing here?" Stone wasn't sure they'd come to do him in or save him. But when Raspberry lifted her SMG and aimed at the small box that controlled the steel bands which held Stone in place and fired—he knew that his ass had just been plucked from some non-elective surgery that he would be just as happy to do without.

"I put a tracer on you," she grinned as the lock mechanism burst into pieces. "We followed you all the way down here staying back about ten miles or so so no one—not even you—would know. We been battling these bastards for too long, decided it was time to make our move. Guess we came at the right time."

"You can't even begin to imagine how close," Stone said with incredible relief as he sat up and rubbed his bleeding wrists.

"Free these other poor bastards," the biker queen commanded her troops. Another six bikes came roaring in from another side of the room and continued past them, hunting down anything that moved.

"I thought you were after me," Stone said as he jumped up and ripped off the uniform of a dead attendant lying on the floor and started dressing himself.

"I cooled the sisters down. Told them it was our chance to follow you in and take the bastards out. Totally and completely like you would burn out a hornet's nest. In a way, Stone, you were the best thing that happened to my power struggle for control of the Ballbusters for years. And a good fuck too. Want to have a quick one?" she added slyly as she watched his flesh disappear behind a greenshirt jumpsuit.

Stone grinned with dumb embarrassment in spite of the carnage around them. He rushed over to Excaliber, who was just coming out himself, the gas that had been pumped into him already wearing off. Stone freed him and got the dog to its feet where it stood unsteadily. It didn't look any worse for wear. The pit bull had the same magic marker strokes where Kerhausen had been about to make his cuts. Letting the animal get its sea legs, Stone rushed to the far table where the half man/half woman was struggling within its confines. Raspberry handed Stone her SMG and four clips, taking out another from behind her seat. Stone fired out the lock system on the woman/man and helped it to its feet.

"What the hell is that?" Raspberry asked with disgust at the rotting sewed-up sexual mutilation.

"Dr. Kerhausen has been cutting up people down here for years," Stone said, having to turn his nose away from the stench of the rotting flesh on the person. Suddenly there was a rattling noise on the floor beneath one of the operating tables and Stone reached out and grabbed a bent-over figure trying to make a getaway.

"Doctor," Stone said with a grim smile. "How fortunate I've found you."

"Please," the doctor said. "I'm extremely wealthy. I have gold and silver hidden all over the country. I can make you the richest man in America overnight. And you," the doctor begged as he turned to the biker queen covered in leather and studs.

"This is the scum who did all this?" Raspberry asked, her face clouded with rage.

"This is him—Hitler's personal physician. And the Dwarf's as well. The man's been around."

"Not any longer," she said, lifting her weapon.

"No, no," Stone said sharply, putting his hand out and

pushing the SMG away. He turned to the dying man/woman. "He's yours—can you—handle it?"

"Yesss, I cannnn," the rotting mutilation hissed out through its woman's lips that were too small for its mouth so that when it talked blood oozed from the cracked skin. "Leeave him wittthh meeee."

"Will do," Stone said softly as the six other biker women stood by silently. As tough and battle-hardened as they were none had ever seen anything like this. Stone and Raspberry grabbed hold of the squirming doctor and slammed him down onto one of the empty operating tables. They closed the metal wrist and ankle bands around him and then stood back as the man/woman thing lurched over to the table. Stone watched as the thing caught its breath and looked down into the terrified eyes of the doctor. And somewhere in that twisted, scarred, infected face something smiled and gave Stone and Raspberry a look of thanks. Then it reached for a scalpel lying along the edge of the table and dug in. And Kerhausen's screams began.

Stone walked away from the table wanting to let him/her do its thing in private. The biker women mounted their bikes as those they had freed who could still walk or move at all lurched off towards the table where Kerhausen was being butchered.

"Thanks," Stone said to Raspberry as he saw mixed looks of desire and hate on the other women's faces. They didn't all like the fact that they had saved him. But it hardly mattered now. He was alive. "What are your plans?"

"We're going for their main weapons depot, which we have a map of—level 16. Also trying to free whatever women prisoners we can who are trapped in this place. We've got time bombs set for one hour from now. So be out of here by then, because this whole fucking place is going to go up like Mount Vesuvius, you hear me?"

"Hear you," Stone echoed back, slamming a fresh clip into the 9mm autopistol. It felt damned good to be holding it in his hands. If nothing else at least he'd be able to go out fighting like he wanted, instead of on that table. He shuddered to even consider what almost happened. Suddenly, impulsively, not giving a shit what the other "girls" thought, Stone put his hands around Raspberry's shoulders, pulled her face forward and planted a hard kiss on her lips. She didn't seem to give a shit what the others thought either because she returned the gesture, and the two of them stood there in the middle of the carnage grappling for a good ten seconds. Then they parted.

"See you, Stone," she said, jumping onto the top of her bike. And like that she started up and was gone, tearing down the corridor sending everything in her path shooting off against the walls. These women were out for coon today. Stone was glad he was on their side. He heard wrenching screams and glanced over to see the man/woman cutting into a line it had drawn around the doctor's pelvic area. Apparently he/she had some transplant ideas of its own.

CHAPTER
Twenty-three

STONE tore out of "surgery" with bloodlust in his eyes. He had been praying to have this opportunity from the moment he had been captured. The dog too was pissed off as hell, running alongside him, snarling up a storm. Bodies already lay all over the place as the Ballbusters left a trail of human and mechanical flotsam and jetsam in their wake. Sirens were starting to go off everywhere and as he rounded a turn in the corridor Stone was suddenly confronted by a whole slew of greenshirts with their SMGs at the ready. They didn't hesitate but let loose with a barrage of fire as Stone dove to the floor. They didn't see the dog, as their instantaneous reactions had been primed to human level. And the pit bull tore straight ahead, slamming into the leg of one teeth first so he and the dog went flying backwards.

Before the greenshirts could quite get themselves together Stone was unleashing his own migration of 9mm birds who flew into flesh. Three of them went back and down, the fourth trying to get a bead on Stone, who had run out of ammo and was slamming another clip into the pistol Raspberry had given him. The guard ripped his SMG around but before the command could go from brain to finger to pull the trigger he suddenly jerked forward, a spray of blood shooting up all around his head. As the

SMG flew from his hands the guard was slammed down into the steel floor face first as Excaliber bit down with everything he had into the man's neck. As they hit the floor the greenshirt's head tipped over at an odd angle as the tendons and muscle along one whole side had been severed. The pit bull spat out the bloody garbage and turned to look at Stone eyes bright lungs heaving, ready for whatever.

"I owe you," Stone shouted down the body-strewn corridor as he slammed the clip all the way in and it made a reassuring click. He jumped on his feet and grabbed one of the SMGs and another load of ammo, and then just ran as fast as his legs could pump, jumping over the bodies like an obstacle course. Stone prayed he would remember all the different levels and intricate pathways of the place that he had memorized from the dwarf woman's map. He must have gone about five hundred yards down the steel corridor and then came to a junction of four halls heading out at right angles. N-1, that was what he wanted; he was sure of it. Stone saw the ghost of his father leering down from the fluorescent tube inset into the ceiling as if to say, don't fuck up, asshole, the fate of the entire world could depend on what you do in the next few minutes.

As if Stone needed any more motivation. He knew what the score was. He heard a whole slew of voices and grabbed the dog, pulling him into a service closet and slamming the door closed. Several dozen booted footsteps came rushing. Stone waited ten seconds until he couldn't hear boots anymore, and then opened the seamless steel door and tore back down the hall. He reached the elevator bank within another hundred yards or so, and debated for a moment whether or not to take the thing. But there was no time to fart around—he had to move fast. The light blinked above one of four elevator doors and Stone stood in front of it as the doors slid silently open.

There were three greenshirts inside, officers by the patches and shit on their chests and shoulders. But medals don't do a hell of a lot of good in blood combat. They went for their sidearms, all still holstered at their side. But Stone was faster, much faster. He let loose with a scythe of slugs that cut right across the elevator at gut level. All three went flying backwards against the wall, their stomachs bleeding profusely from numerous holes. Stone jumped into the elevator as Excaliber hesitated outside, not liking the idea of being holed up with the bodies in such a tight space. But the sudden appearance of another squad of guards just around the bend drove the dog forward. It shot inside just as the doors slammed shut inches behind its tail. Stone could hear the sharp metallic sounds of scores of slugs slamming into the outer elevator door. But it didn't matter, they were already going down—down to the deepest level of the NAUASC subterranean city—the Dwarf's chambers.

After about five seconds of descent a bong sounded electronically and the doors slid open. Stone expected there would be guards outside and he came out firing, pulling the trigger and spraying in every direction before he even quite knew what was what. And it wasn't a bad idea. Four men on each side of the doors had been waiting, waiting a second too long. Screams and blood filled the air as a few of them managed to get off their own return fire. Stone felt a sharp burning pain tear through his right shoulder and he ripped the SMG, taking out the shooter in a withering blast of fire right into the man's face, which disintegrated into red mush. The greenshirt did a weird backflip right through the air before landing on top of his head, which cracked open on the hard metal floor.

Stone kept firing until the clip was done. He ripped it out, muzzle smoking and slammed in another, eyes darting back and forth wildly. But not a mouse was stirring.

"Come on, dog," Stone hissed as he moved forward low. "Keep your teeth sharp." But the dog didn't need any advice in that direction as its jaws kept opening and closing instinctively, ready to sink into anything that moved. Stone tore down the main corridor, trying to visualize the map the dwarf woman had given him, doubtless now back with his clothes which had been scalpeled from him in Dr. Kerhausen's medical room. He should have stopped and picked the damned thing up. That was stupid. But everything had been moving so fast. He sure as hell wasn't strolling back now.

He came to the end of the corridor and the thing split, one going right, one left. He stood for a moment trying to decide but Excaliber suddenly barked several times and headed toward the left, turning around as if to see what was taking Chow Boy so fucking long. Couldn't he smell that the Dwarf was just ahead? Couldn't he sense the foul odor of the ugly thing, the scent that oozed from its stumps?

"You know where you're going, dog, so let's go." The animal started forward as if on a track meet, glad to see that the Chow Boy had at least a little common sense, if a fatal lack of smarts. Stone ran, hardly able to keep up with the panting beast, which seemed to know exactly where it was heading. The corridor was nearly two hundred feet long, and by the time they reached the metal door at the end they had picked up some pretty good speed. Excaliber was not one for knocking—or even using the handle—he flew into it with such force that the whole thing shook slightly. The animal fell back on its back dazed, its legs quivering in the air like an overturned turtle.

Stone knew a better way to get in. He reached out and slammed the seven digit code number into the keypad built in the steel door, the code that the dwarf woman had given him, she being the only one that the Dwarf trusted to clean his pad. A mistake he was about to pay for dearly. The door slid open just as the pitbull got groggily to its feet, wondering dimly if it had been such a good idea after all to charge into the steel door. Maybe next time—

Stone was already inside as the animal pondered. He rushed several steps inside the huge chamber that stretched off ahead and his eyes stopped like they'd been frozen with Magic Glue as he stared toward the right side of the room. For there, tied down naked to a bed with her legs spread apart was his sister. The Dwarf had rigged up some insane kind of contraption right above her, a whining pulley system with levers and straps and all kinds of madness which had been built into a steel frame erected over the bed. It was easy to see just what the little slime had in mind: to deflower April by lowering himself mechanically from the top. He was stabbing away with one of his arm stumps at a set of dials to his right and the entire rig was lowering his miniature twisted naked body right down on top of the dazed, drugged woman.

"Jesus, mother of God," Stone muttered under his breath, so repulsed by the sight that he stood totally frozen for the sheerest second paralyzed with horror. The Dwarf was only inches from making his consummation real.

"Dwwaaaarrrrfffff!" Stone screamed out with every bit of rage that burned within him. The yellow eggman's eyes suddenly darted up as he saw his mortal enemy.

"You bastard, you're dead. You must be dead. You can't ruin everything," he shrieked like a rusty hinge, slamming even harder at the controls of the pulley system to go down so that he could impregnante her with his freak child.

"Nooooo!" Stone screamed as he rushed forward, not daring to fire as he might easily hit April as well. "Noooooooo!" The Dwarf suddenly realized he was't going to make it—and in the choice between producing the heir to his throne or saving his own wretched life, the Dwarf without hesitation chose the latter. He pressed another button on the panel, cursing under his breath as he gave Stone a look of sheerest hatred.

"You die now!" he hissed. "We all die!" Suddenly he was rocketed over onto his side, the whole pulley contraption turning and depositing him right into his wheelchair, which sat next to the bed. In a flash he was stabbing away with both stumps at the twin machine guns built into the arm rests on each side. A stream of white hot slugs peppered the room. But both Stone and Wonderdog had already hit the dirt.

"You've brought this on the world, Martin Stone," the

Dwarf screamed. "A hundred missiles will rain down on the planet Earth. What is the sound of total annhiliation, Stone?" he laughed, and even as Stone rose up to sight the zooming chair up with his SMG, a surface of the wall opened and in a flash the Dwarf was through it as it ripped shut behind him.

"Oh God no," Stone whispered, his face drained of blood as he rose to his feet. He walked quickly back to April and looked down at her. She was in a total daze, even more drugged out than she'd been the night before at the banquet. Stone saw barely a trace of light in her eyes. But as he kept looking down into her sweat-coated face he saw her lips move almost imperceptibly.

"Martin, Martin, thank God," she whispered as soft as a dove's wings fluttering.

CHAPTER

Twenty-four

"**C**OME on, baby," Stone said as he freed her and then found some clothes so she could cover herself. She seemed to be coming out of it just a little, at least she seemed to recognize Stone as she just kept whispering "Martin, Martin, Martin," over and over again like some sort of prayer to protect her against all the horror that she'd undergone.

"It's okay now," Stone lied to her as he put shoes on her limp feet. "You're safe, April, it's all over." The dog kept sniffing at the insane pulley contraption over the bed and suddenly snapped at it hard, taking a dislike to the machinery involved. It took only a few rips for the pit bull to pull the whole side of the thing apart, as joints bent with a squeaking sound and suddenly the whole thing toppled over and hit the floor with a thundering crash. April's eyes jerked up wildly at the sound. But Stone stroked her as a small smile crossed over his face. At least the dog had awakened her.

Suddenly he heard what sounded like engines and two of the Ballbusters came screeching through the opened door he had just come through.

"Stone, it's you," one of them shouted, and Stone realized it was Raspberry. It was hard to tell at first as blood was streaming down the whole side of her face. Still, she was riding her bike and talking, so it couldn't be too bad. "I was just making a final sweep for any of my girls. We're getting out of here man. The place is going to blow in sixteen minutes. You need a ride?"

"No, not yet," Stone said. "I've got to try to stop the Dwarf—he's headed for the missile room to launch the whole fucking sky full of Star Wars missiles down on the Earth—down on this place. Take April, though. Get her out of here, then all of you just get away fast. I'll—do my best. If I don't make it out could—"

"Don't worry about it," Raspberry replied, looking him in the eye. "She'll be taken care of, I promise you."

"Thanks," he said wearily and then turned down the corridor as the biker queen got April on the back of her Harley and pulled the girl's arms around her waist.

"Hold on sugar, we're going for a ride like you've never been on."

"Martin, Martin," April just kept moaning but held on firmly as the bike screamed out its gasoline roar and headed back out of the Dwarf's chambers. Stone knew there was one final level below this—the missile command center. The map had indicated fire stairs at the far side of this level. He ran over more oozing dead bodies—the work of the biker chicks. They didn't take any prisoners. And three dead Ballbusters were mixed in with the carnage.

Stone hit the fire stairs on the run, spraying a burst inside the doorway. But no one was on the other side. Above him he could hear the motorcycles as the Ballbusters were driving right up the stairs as they had come down. With the dog at his heels Stone edged down the two flights to the final level. The steel door that had stood at the entrance was blown right off its hinges—and two more Ballbusters lay around their twisted bikes, blood coating everything like a squeezed jelly donut. They'd tried to get in down here—and hadn't.

"Dog, it's kiss your ass goodbye time, you understand pal," Stone said, whispering to the dog as he checked his

SMG. A final clip and one in the 9mm and that was it. "'Cause we got to go in there, whatever's happening. It's been fun," Stone said, reaching down and giving a quick scratch behind the animal's ear. The dog looked up with a strained expression as if to say—please Chow Boy, emotion is for peacetime—it's fighting time now. They charged down the stairs leaping over the bikes and the dead and tore through the charred frame.

There were greenshirts waiting, a good dozen of them hidden around the floor. But they weren't quite ready for action, thinking that the roar of the bikers' engines meant that the enemy were splitting. And that was their last mistake. For Stone came in firing from both hands before they could even react. It was like *Bad Day at Black Rock* and *Gunfight at the OK Corral* all rolled into one, with slugs flying everywhere into greenshirts. The pit bull ran hugging the wall, then flew up on a shirt starting to get a bead on Stone, and slashed the side of his face down to the bone. When they had both passed not one guard was left untouched.

Just beyond was the main computer center—the brain of the entire missile defense system. Stone's jaw hung open as he came tearing in. The place was as big as two football fields and absolutely filled to overflow with beeping and blinking radar and computers, monitors and readouts, rows of screens showing the view of the Earth from the missiles' point of view in space, twenty-thousand miles above the Earth. It all could be seen displayed out in acres of command post equipment. This must have been the center of the entire space fleet, Stone realized. And the Dwarf had control of it. Surely the gods had gone mad.

He ran down the huge complex firing at everything, including technicians at various posts. And his slugs rocked them from their seats. Anyone who was trying to blow up the world was fair game in Stone's book and he didn't hesitate to blow every bastard he could see right out of his chair. Bullets tore into the screens and control panels as Stone left a smoking sparking trail behind him and small fires which broke out here in there in the circuitries. Excaliber took up shotgun and keeping an eye on anything that moved, taking out a pistol hand that reached from a shadow. The hand still gripping the gun fell to the floor. The pit bull didn't look back.

Suddenly Stone saw him ahead—the Dwarf, racing down a row of control panels in his wheelchair, punching out with his stumps at rows of buttons and dials with an absolutely maniacal expression on his face. Stone prayed it wasn't already too late, that this wasn't the final launch sequence that Dwarf was punching in right now. He ran down the central aisle of the place firing, holding the trigger and letting loose with a barrage. The Dwarf heard the cracks and turned his wheelchair on a dime, both of the twin machine guns on the armrests opening up. They came right at each other, two men, one representing the darkness, the other the light, snarling with hate, guns blazing. Then Stone took a hit as a slug tore right through his left thigh. He went down in a tumble of hands and legs and slammed hard into the side of a table, letting out a quick scream from the intense pain. Excaliber dove behind an immense blinking computer as a dozen slugs ripped into the steel floor just behind him, leaving gouged-out, smoking little craters.

The Dwarf laughed shrilly and came forward from about fifty feet off, his guns continuing to smoke as two rows of slugs raced toward Stone's prone body. "Die Stone, die!" the Dwarf screamed, wanting more than anything to take out this bastard who had ruined his wedding night. The bullets were inches from Stone when a shape hurtled down from one of the cross beams that were built all over the place holding lights, racks, screens. This was a human shape falling—the dwarf woman, Elizabeth. And she was holding an immense butcher knife stolen from the kitchen, used to hack up whole cows.

She slammed into the Dwarf, landing on his lap just as the wheelchair came beneath her.

"You!" the Dwarf hissed in real amazement that he had

been betrayed by one so lowly, such a slave of no meaning as the woman who raised her muscular arms high.

"Me!" she laughed back, slamming the sixteen inch blade deep into his scrawny chest. "Me—the dwarf bitch. The worm, the cockroach of NAUASC. Me, Dwarf. And who is the powerful one now?" She stabbed again and then again and again with furious rage, no longer impotent. The dwarf's whole upper body was carved right from the bones like a badly butchered piece of meat, everything hanging down, bones shattered and all. He lost control of the wheelchair as he let loose with a long shrill scream that made the hair on the back of Stone's neck stand on end. Then the wheelchair crashed into a steel wall.

Yet he still heard the dwarf woman's knife, the screams and gurglings of the Dwarf. After another ten seconds there was no more sound. Stone sat up and checked his leg. It was bleeding good, but the bullet didn't seem to have penetrated any arteries. He tied a tourniquet around the top of the leg with a piece of material from a dead tech's shirt. He was able to walk, limping along. Excaliber jumped from behind the table where he had taken up refuge and trotted warily alongside Stone, snarling and showing all his teeth as the two of them approached the overturned wheelchair.

Stone could see a big puddle of blood spreading out from beneath. He reached over and pulled the wheelchair back with some difficulty, as it weighed a ton. But suddenly it dislodged and fell over on its back. Stone gasped. Both of them were dead. Elizabeth's hands were still clutched around the knife which was sunk to the hilt into the Dwarf's chest. She had split the whole back of her head open in the fall, slamming into the side of the steel table. It was cracked like an egg with most of her brains already on the floor around her. Yet she looked happy, almost serene with a smile on her now cooling face. She had done it, she had killed the death freak that no man had been able to kill. And there was a great satisfaction, even unto death, for that accomplishment.

Stone reached over in spite of himself, and touched the

Dwarf to make sure he was dead. The little eggman had escaped death seemingly miraculously in the past. Stone realized he had almost begun to believe the little fucker was immortal. But he was dead all right this time. There was no mistaking it, not with his ribs cut open and his heart and lungs all slashed to pieces. Not with most of him spreading down onto the floor like cheap peanut butter dripping from the edge of the jar. The eyes were open staring straight ahead. And they looked afraid. A look Stone had never seen on the Dwarf before. Elizabeth had even managed to coax that emotion from him at the very end. She had done more than she had realized.

Stone hobbled down the aisle as fast as his wounded leg could carry him, firing at the panels, blowing up everything he saw. He looked up at the displays of the missiles' video system from space as the computers kept showing their angles and trajectories for firing down at Earth. It looked bad—but he didn't know how to interpret it for sure. Stone looked at a clock on the wall as he reached the end of the aisle, leaving everything smoking and blowing up behind him. There was one minute left before bye-bye time if the biker chicks' bombs went off. And somehow he thought they would. He glanced around the command level searching for a way out, an elevator. Suddenly he saw a red sign with the letters "Emergency Rocket Escape" on a wall.

"Come on, dog," Stone screamed at the pit bull, which had jumped up on a table and was starting to gulp down a left-behind sandwich.

"Oh Christ," Stone said with disgust. "Eating even as armageddon approaches. Let's move, dog," he bellowed as he hobbled for all he was worth toward the rocket sign. The pit bull gulped the fake ham and swiss on rye down in a single gulp and reached Stone in three quick leaps. Stone saw a glass window like a fire alarm in the old days. "Break In Case of Emergency." He reached out with the butt of his SMG and slammed at the glass, then pushed the broken pieces away and pressed a large red button that sat ominously inside.

The steel door on the wall slid open and Stone stepped a little nervously into the telephone-booth-sized room as the dog slithered in between his legs and sat down disgruntled about having to get into such a small space again, as that was all it seemed to be doing lately, crawling into its own coffin.

"Hold onto the grips at your side," a mechanical sounding voice spoke over a speaker hidden above his head. "Ejection time ten seconds."

"Hold on to your fur, dog," Stone screamed down as he felt the whole thing start vibrating like it was thinking of erupting. "We're about to ride the Cyclone at Coney Island and the bomb blast at Hiroshima all rolled into one."

CHAPTER
Twenty-five

STONE felt the rocket system ignite beneath him as the steel-walled cylindrical booth trembled as if in an earthquake. He felt the heat and then the jarring rush of super acceleration as he hit four g's in one second. And suddenly he found himself being squeezed down and hardly able to breathe. The rocket shot up a steel tube with a tail of smoke rushing behind. Stone thought his ears as well as his chest would burst. The pressure was tremendous. And even as they rose the rocket seemed to fire harder, accelerating as it climbed. Stone felt like he was being crushed. His head fell onto his chest and pressed hard against it. He saw Excaliber on the floor of the rocket booth, flattened like a rug, his mouth wide open and huffing for air.

They then burst free of the ground and there was a sudden great change of pressure as Stone felt his ears pop. They rose for about four more seconds and Stone could see through a crack in the side, damaged when they rose, that they were up about five hundred feet above the ground. Below he could see the ruins, the wreckage above ground stretching off for miles. There was a second small explosion above and Stone felt the whole escape shell jerk hard as a parachute billowed up overhead.

The instant the parachute snapped open the pressure was

released on his lungs and he could breathe again. Excaliber as well took in a long breath and then let out with a pissed-off yowl. Even as he went to take in a second breath of sweet oxygen Stone saw the ground below him turn yellow and orange. The very earth seemed to be rent asunder as flames rocketed out from numerous fissures in the ground. It was as if a volcano were being born as gas and fire shot up everywhere, creating multiple chasms in the earth from the pressure of the explosions below.

"Oh God no," Stone whispered as he felt the surge of heat from the flames. But even as he thought he had bought it and his blood drained from his cheeks he felt the chute lift them and then they were being buffeted around in the air. Suddenly they were being bounced inside the booth like someone shaking dice in a cup, spinning around in the air as the heat currents sent the chute all over the place. They rose to about seven hundred feet and then shot fast toward the south. Then they were coming down again, only it was too fast. Stone looked through a crack in the metal ceiling—the chute was aflame above them. The ground loomed up brown and filled with shattered concrete and then even as Stone knew they were coming in much too fast, they hit. And he fell into peaceful darkness.

"Martin, Martin, please wake up." It was April and she was calling him. He was in heaven. His mother and father were standing there. And she was with them too and they were all smiling. But Stone wasn't sure he wanted to embrace them as the flesh was falling from their faces and blood oozed from their reaching hands. No he didn't want to, didn't want to—

"Martin, it's April. Open your eyes—you're alive." Stone opened his eyes slowly and saw faces above him. They weren't his parents. April and Raspberry were looking down at him with concern. His head ached like it was on fire. Everything burned.

"What—what—" he stuttered as he rose to a sitting position. The escape booth he had ridden in lay shattered all around them. God only knew how he had survived the fall. The dog, needless to say, was up and about sniffing the air, searching for food scents and waiting for Chow Boy to get his act together.

"The chute was pushed a few hundred feet," Raspberry said as she brightened, seeing that he was actually alive. "But it caught on fire. We were on a hill and saw you come out. Figured it was the Dwarf and came cruising to take him into never-never land. But—it's you." Stone stood up, on very wobbly legs. The bleeding on his tourniqueted leg had slowed to a medium ooze. He needed emergency repairs, maybe a full overhaul and about a year of R&R. None of which were too likely.

Suddenly he remembered. How could he forget? The Dwarf had pushed all the damn buttons on the missile command. His eyes lifted to the sky. It was late afternoon and the heavens were slate gray like it was going to rain forever once it began. He couldn't see any traces of missile flame, or glint of incoming nose cone. But then there might not have been time—yet. It had only been ten, maybe fifteen minutes since—

"We better get the hell out of here," Raspberry said, hopping up on her bike. "Come on, Stone. There could be more secondaries from below. This whole area could go up." Flames were shooting from several square acres now as the ground ripped to pieces and disappeared into burning fissures. Below he could see the crumbled levels, all fallen together like a deck of steel cards. Everything within was being churned in the flaming walls of moving steel and concrete, ground up into powder that glowed red-hot. Nothing could have survived below. Not even a germ.

"No, you go," Stone said. "Me and my sister will stay and see what happens. I'm tired of running. If the end is coming, I want to be standing looking it in the face like a man. It sounds crazy; I won't even begin to deny it, but—"

"I hear you, Stone," Raspberry said. "Well, there's a couple of gassed up bikes over there. Some of the girls didn't make it. A lot of them didn't. Still, we set out what we wanted to accomplish."

"I owe you," Stone said, looking over the eight Ballbusters who had lived through the attack, a third of their original number. "And my sister, as well. Neither of us would be alive—but for you. And if the world has the slightest chance of surviving it will be because of all of you. We'll know damned soon enough." He raised his eyes again to the skies thinking he saw a shape and feeling his heart speed up. But it was just a flock of birds flying fast and low like they wanted to get the hell out of there themselves.

"Hope we get to fuck again some day," Raspberry smirked, throwing her blond hair back and sliding on her steel helmet. "Adios amigo," She turned the accelerator of her Harley and the bikers tore off after her, bouncing over the wreckage as they followed in v-formation behind their Queen.

Stone stood up, pain ripping through his body. He supported himself for a moment on April's shoulder. Their eyes met and she seemed clearer now, if still very tired, hardly able to move or talk. But her eyes, they were definitely clearer.

"Thanks," she said, leaning over and kissing him on the cheek. "If we're to die, I can stand it if it's here and now —with you. We can join Mom and Dad, and—" Though the words were sad and made Stone feel like bursting into tears, her face was strong, eyes unafraid of the coming night. Stone wasn't sure he was quite as unafraid. But it was true—at least they were together. His long search was over. He put his arm around her shoulder and they stood there staring at the skies, as the dog relieved itself on a jagged piece of concrete tilted sideways as big as the side of a house. Stone gazed up into the gathering clouds like a madman searching for sanity. And he waited and prayed and winced at every little shape that seemed to form up along the churning cloud line.

* * *

The earth was turned into a glowing powder that spread out through the solar system, blown by the atomic winds. In the orbit where the noble planet, third from the sun— and considered by many to be the most beautiful of the star system—had spun for billions of years, was now only a cloud of luminous dust and rocks that sparkled like murderous diamonds in the heavens, a beacon, a lighthouse signal to the rest of the universe for all time to come that an intelligent species had made all the wrong choices.